EYES IN THE DARK

ROWENA DAWN

SCARLET LEAF

2017

This is a work of fiction. Names, characters, places and incidents are products of the author's imagination and are not to be construed as real. Any resemblance to actual events, locales, organizations or persons, living or dead, is entirely coincidental.

SCARLET LEAF
TORONTO
ONTARIO
CANADA
COPYRIGHT BY ROWENA DAWN
ISBN: 978-1-988397-17-7

For information address Scarlet Leaf Publishing House at:
scarletleafpublishinghouse@gmail.com

TO CORINA AND EMIL

PROLOGUE

A thin crowd surrounded the casket and not because of the cold spring rain, which had been pouring for the last twelve hours. Not many people had attended the church service either.

'A funeral in the middle of the week will do that to you,' Diane shook her head with grief. People had jobs and families. She couldn't blame them for their absence.

The pastor's words flew past her ears. She'd never been a religious person and didn't find any comfort in the ritual now, either.

When Diane's eyes had swept over the faces of the few people inside the church just moments before, her heart had tightened. Bad luck had taken away her aunt's chance at having the people she'd known for years at her side on this last day.

The late Martha Elgin had been well known and respected in the county. '*I never even imagined so many people loved her*,' Diane thought and wiped her tears.

The constant string of people, coming to pay their respects during the last three nights of the wake, had impressed Diane MacLean, Martha's only niece.

She only realized the priest had ended the service when people began to move and file before Diane to present their whispered condolences and regrets once again.

Some squeezed her hand with affection while others hugged her, although they'd known her for only a few days. Afterwards, they left the cemetery, huddled under big umbrellas.

They would come to the house later, where Diane, with the help of a catering company, had prepared a last repast in her aunt's honor, scheduled for three in the afternoon.

Soon however, Diane remained alone near the casket, her eyes misty with tears, while two burly young men were waiting impatiently under the canopy of a big oak. They wanted to finish with the burial and find some shelter inside, away from the rain. Their eyes laid squarely on her, willing her to leave already.

Diane whispered her farewell and touched the lid of the black lacquered casket with a shaky hand. She loved her aunt and regretted she hadn't come to visit her for almost three years already. Now, her words fell on deaf ears.

She nodded toward the grave diggers and followed the stone path leading out of the cemetery and to the parking lot. She failed to notice the three men hidden in the shadow of a cluster of trees behind her.

The tallest leaned forward and whispered a few words. Nodding, one of the other two made his way through the trees to the same parking lot.

The man beat Diane to the punch. Comfortably seated in his car, he watched her coming up the trail slowly.

She seemed tired and didn't care about the rain, even though her umbrella didn't shield her very well. The remote look in her eyes betrayed her scattered thoughts.

Diane didn't notice the man in the car. She placed the umbrella in the trunk of her SUV and hurried to the driver's side.

She drove away, oblivious to the other car, which was trailing her closely now. She drove under the speed limit, although she was expected in town. Her aunt's lawyer had invited her to the reading of the will.

'I already told him I might be late. What's the rush after all? The will won't change.'

CHAPTER 1

The air tumbled in his lungs and he tasted the smell of the earlier rain in the air. The smell of wet leaves, rustled by the wind all over the forest floor, invigorated him.

He watched the woman closely from underneath the shade of the trees where he'd found a good spot to hide.

'It's just a necessity,' he lied to himself. He knew he liked what he saw. His imagination already roamed on paths he knew he should have avoided.

He held still, afraid he would make a noise by stepping on the twigs that littered the floor of the forest and give his position away. He had enough time to make his presence known and didn't want to scare her before the time was right. He'd outlined a plan and never strayed from a well-thought-out plan.

His eyes roved over the woman's body. Her neck arched and reminded him of a deer at a watering hole at dawn, sniffing the air to feel the hunter lurking.

He grinned. *'Yep, sweetheart, you sense me here, but you're not sure. Yet.'*

Fatigue had etched visible lines at the corner of her eyes and around her mouth. He'd been watching her for a few hours now and had seen her working hard as she tried to put the ranch house to rights.

The wind teased him with a faint whiff of green apples and lemon, stirring long-forgotten memories. He bristled and scowled the memories away.

The woman shivered and rubbed her arms. The night air was getting cooler.

Her rich coppery hair hung in a messy ponytail. Wisps of hair framed her face and made her look vulnerable.

Suddenly, the man decided he'd watched his fill. *'Show time,'* he said under his breath and stepped out from his hiding place.

"Hey, you over there!"

She almost jumped a feet up when the rough voice whipped through the air. It came from the left side of the yard where lots of bushes and tall trees darkened the night even more. Her wide eyes turned there and caught the glimpse of a tall shadow moving in the dark and a flash of fear seized her breath.

The man closed the distance between them, a grin in the corner of his mouth. Something close to satisfaction bubbled in his veins.

Her eyes widened even more when his tall and broad shape seemed to engulf the space. The fear in her eyes stirred an unknown emotion deep inside him. He tried to label it, but came out empty.

He ruled out compassion although he couldn't explain why. It wasn't as if he had even remembered how compassion felt like.

For a few tense moments, they stared at each other intensely. Neither one moved.

Fear flickered in her green eyes again. A huge male was striding through her yard as if he'd owned the damn place.

His steely black eyes reflected his innate boldness, laced with a hint of amusement and a feral sliver of unidentified hunger. That hunger troubled her. She didn't care about his amusement or anything else.

They assessed each other like two swordsmen.

'Why the heck didn't I listen to my instincts?' She'd thought herself alone out there at the small ranch house, yet, all evening, she had the feeling that someone was watching her. The sensation had electrified the fine hair at the nape of her neck but she'd foolishly dismissed it.

The ranch was far from any crowded roads, which was fine with her. She didn't need legions of people around and she didn't miss the noises of a big city.

Since the death of her aunt, a few months before, she'd been thinking of moving out of town and making a life for herself there, in the middle of nowhere. A week ago, she'd finally done it. Now, she doubted she'd made the right decision.

"I've got a gun, right here," she shouted at him. Her voice shook. "And I know how to use it," she continued in a shrilling voice. Fear almost smothered her and she hardly pushed the words out of her mouth.

His brash laughter reached her ears and her blood ran cold. *'He doesn't believe me,'* she thought with a shock and for a fleeting moment, she regretted she hadn't taken those self-defense classes she'd been thinking about back then when she was living in the city. *'Well, too bad. It's too late to cry over spilled milk now. Time to face the music.'*

"Yeah, I bet you do," he hollered back, laughing louder. "Sweetheart," he drawled, and honey dripped off his lips, betraying a specific southern accent, "I'm sure you could darn shoot me if you wanted to. But I doubt you do," he continued and lifted an eyebrow, as if he'd dared her. "I just want help for one night, maybe two, tops," he lied boldly through his teeth.

His fake sweet voice made her fear step aside. Anger took its place and climbed up to her lips at his biting sarcasm.

"Town's in that direction," she replied, pointing to his left. "There, you can find all the help you want, mister," she added in clipped words. "There's nothing here for you," she clarified with a sharp gesture.

"I don't feel like going into town right now," he shrugged. "I'm tired. I've been walking long enough. My car broke down a few miles back down that road, and I need a place to stay. I think I like this one," he said in a flat voice, which brought shivers along her spine.

Then, he came closer and under the spot of light from the veranda.

"How dare you?" she pushed through her tight lips with difficulty. Her hands fisted and her nails bit into her palms.

He was rather tall, a bit too tall for her taste. If he'd been shorter, she might have had a chance to fight him back. He was also much heavier than she was. His build reminded her of a fighter. *'This guy's bad news, Diane,'* she thought.

"Be a good Christian girl," he said sweetly. "You won't let a poor man outside in the night, here, in the forest, to fend for himself alone, cold and hungry, will you now?" he asked her with a charming smile and opened his arms wide, taunting her.

"I certainly would," she replied and braced her hands on her hips.

She wanted him to understand his words wouldn't move her. She wasn't a simpleton. The times when people opened their doors to strangers were long gone. Anyway, she was a city girl. That habit wasn't in her make-up.

He stepped closer and reached the stairs of the veranda, undeterred by her refusal. He braced one arm on the handrail. His smiling eyes assessed her resolve.

His eyes pleaded innocence, yet she could read toughness behind his smile. She knew he was far from what he wanted her to believe.

The man was built like the rangers she'd read about. Over six feet tall, his eyes were on the same level with hers, even though he was at the foot of the stairs. His shoulders were broad enough to carry her away if he felt like it.

'Oh boy, oh boy,' she mumbled in her mind. She had to do something and get rid of him.

'Damn my urge to admire the night. If I'd been inside, at least I'd have had a door between this bear of a man and me... Although I don't think a locked door would make too much of a difference if he wanted

in,' she thought, her eyes taking in the rough maleness before them.

"Come on, missy, don't be a bitch," he tried to cajole her. "I need only one bed for the night," he tried to persuade her, always with that smile, which got on her nerves. "I promise it won't be yours," he added.

She noticed his smile never reached his eyes. The man's eyes were two black arrows trained on her, surveying her every movement. Chips of ice sparkled inside his dark pupils, chilling her to the bone.

His evident sarcasm crawled on her skin and his nonchalant attitude scared her more because she didn't understand his game.

"Are you crazy or what?" she replied with anger in her voice.

"Or what, I think," he softly answered back.

"How could you think I'd let you sleep in my house?" she said furiously.

'It's like she wants to spit on me and be done with me,' he mused. *'Not so easily*

done, honey. The game's over when I say it's over. Now, be a good girl and give in. I won't bother you… too much.'

"All right, then your barn, what about that?" he offered a compromise.

'It's not like I can't afford it for the moment. You'll play a different tune tomorrow, honey.'

"You can lock your doors tonight, and tomorrow, we'll talk some more. What are you saying? It seems like a good trade to me," he shrugged again and tapped the cowboy hat, he had in his hand, on his thigh.

She didn't like his words and was afraid to think about what sort of trade he was talking about. 'Yeah, like a locked door would stop you from coming in.'

However, she knew she was at a disadvantage. If she wanted to end that ludicrous discussion, she had to accept his offer and hope he would keep to the barn.

"Go to the barn and wait for me," she said brusquely. "I'll bring you some blankets so you won't feel the cold of the night. All right?"

He smiled at her again, but this time, he showed her two rows of perfect, big, white teeth. His smile reminded her of a wolf in front of its prey, and she shivered.

Then, he bowed mockingly and turned around to go to the barn erected on one side of the big yard.

She didn't move until a metallic squeak reached her ears, letting her know he'd opened the rusty barn door.

Then, she ran inside and belatedly locked the door behind her. It was pointless, but she needed that blanket of security for a moment.

She hadn't forgotten she had to go back out there with the blankets she'd promised. She had to give him some food as well. She couldn't do otherwise if she wanted to avoid his coming to the house to ask, but she couldn't make her feet move. Her legs shook so badly that she needed to lean on the wall to keep herself standing.

Finally, the fear that he might come back forced her to move and she climbed the stairs to the second floor. With shaking hands, she took two blankets from the linen cupboard in the hallway upstairs.

Then, she raided the kitchen and prepared three large sandwiches. '*Better safe than sorry,*' she thought.

It took her longer than she expected, but then, she kept dropping things. Her fingers shook and she couldn't control them. She took a can of soda out of the fridge and headed to the front door.

Her heart beat faster. She was so scared that she practically jumped out of her skin. Before opening the door, she cautiously moved the flimsy drapes, which covered the side window, and looked out, carefully.

The light in the barn was on, but she couldn't see anything else. '*I hope he's waiting for me there and not here.*'

Her only other choice was to call the sheriff, but by the time he'd have made it there, she could have been fodder for the vultures.

She opened the door and went out into the dark. In a few long strides, she reached the door of the barn and shouted, "Mister, are you in there?"

The door of the barn opened with a screech, and startled, she jumped back a few steps and screamed.

"Did I startle you?" he asked, mildly interested. His tone showed he didn't care one way or another.

"What do you think?" she scowled at him. "Here are your blankets," she said angrily and shoved the blankets to him.

Then, she turned back, forgetting about the food she still held in her hand. In the corner of her eye, she caught a glimpse of his right brow going up sardonically. She realized he was pointedly eying the sandwiches in her hand and she had the impulse to throw everything to him.

She controlled herself and handed him the food. Afterwards, she turned around again to leave the barn without a word.

"Good night to you too," he said sarcastically, and burst into a hearty laughter. It sounded crazy to her ears.

He knew her imagination had run wild and that was why she behaved like a scared doe.

She mumbled a few choice words she wasn't supposed to know. The words reached the man's ears and his mirth became louder. He was pleased both with the situation and her colorful vocabulary.

She didn't stop. She left the barn in a hurry, but she couldn't help but notice the man's musky scent and something like butterflies fluttered in her stomach. She refused to dwell on that strange sensation and focused on her fury.

She almost ran back to the house. She wanted to put as much distance as possible between her and the giant residing in her barn for the night. She locked the door behind her and breathed with relief when she heard the lock clicking into place.

She gave up on drinking her usual cup of tea before going to bed and went directly upstairs to her bedroom on shaky legs.

She changed into her pajamas although it took her a while. Her fingers shook so hard that she barely could button her blouse.

An owl hooted into the night and the sound filled her with anxiety. It sounded like an omen. She hesitantly went to bed, bothered by bleak thoughts. The feeling that something was about to happen kept her awake for a long time.

CHAPTER 2

The dawn was just coloring the horizon when the man came out of the barn, rubbing his eyes. His mood had soured the night before and never recovered. He admitted that sleeping in a barn hadn't been the best choice for him, and his eyes thundered with ire.

Nature called and he visited the cluster of trees at the back of the yard. *'She wouldn't be too happy if I went inside to look for the bathroom.'*

Coming back, he ruffled his hair with impatient fingers and looked around. His eyes fell on the old well in the yard first, but then he saw that a new water pump had been installed in its proximity.

He stretched at first, to appease the ache in his shoulders, and then, he took off his shirt. Modesty was alien to him. He didn't care if his hostess watched him.

No one had ever described him as being shy, and he knew he had the body to offer a good show for free to the woman in the house.

'After all, it's nothing but fair game to pay her back for making me sleep in the barn.'

He planned on making her pay dearly for her mistrust, although deep down, he knew she was in the right. No woman in the world, even one with only a few functioning brain cells, would have welcomed an unknown man into her house at night.

Still, the woman had hurt his pride. Darn it all! He didn't look like a criminal. Yes, he'd walked for a few hours and he'd been dusty.

He'd intended to be there late in the morning, but the dang car broke down and he couldn't do anything about it. The battery had finally given out and nothing he tried revived it. No cars had passed by and he had waited there close to two hours. So, no help from that corner.

A film of dust and sweat covered him when he finally arrived on her doorstep. He'd marched a long way from the other end of the forest to that God forsaken place.

'I even wore my best pair of jeans and my favorite shirt in her honor. And she looked at me like I was a piece of shit,' he thought and scowled, not caring if the woman was wary of his appearance on her steps.

While he was washing his neck and strong muscular arms at the pump, she watched him from behind the curtains. Her eyes swept over the expanse of his muscular back and a tinge of attraction fluttered in her belly.

She'd known immediately when he woke up. Maybe the screech of the barn door had woken her. Or maybe she'd heard his steps in the yard or the water flowing at the pump.

Anyway, she'd gone to the window at once and now she was watching him with something close to fascination.

She refused to analyze her reasons. Her mouth had never watered seeing a handsome body before. *'There's always a first time for everything,'* she mused.

His strong arms showed sculpted muscles and his broad chest, covered with dark coarse hair, glistened with water drops.

She fisted her hands because her fingers ached to brush through that thick hair and she bit her bottom lip. Then, she shook her head, *'Damn it! What are you thinking, woman? Get a grip!'*

She left the window, and headed to the bathroom to take a long shower to wash away her desire for the man she'd locked outside the night before.

Cold water whipped her body and punished her for a few minutes. She welcomed the grueling punishment because she needed her sanity back and fast.

Afterwards, she chose a modest t-shirt and a pair of jeans, which had seen better times. A brief glance in the mirror assured her she was decent enough. She didn't want to raise his eyebrows over her choice of attire. Satisfied, she headed downstairs and unlocked the front door.

He was already there, in front of the door, rubbing his skin with a rough towel he'd taken from the backpack he'd had with him the night before.

She tried hard to take her eyes from his chest. *'Damn! Why am I so obsessed with that damn chest?'*

"If you want breakfast, you may come in," she abruptly said and then, turned her back to him, as if he'd been of no consequence.

She sauntered to the kitchen, apparently uninterested whether he followed her or not.

His eyes zeroed in on her behind snuggled in tight frayed jeans and grinned. He imagined she'd chosen them to stop him looking, but the result was the opposite. His desire ran deep and strong now.

Those might have been some old pants, but they looked perfect on her. They fit her like a second skin. When she moved, they hugged her hips tight and he needed all his ragged control not to jump her.

He laughed at himself and finished drying his body with the towel. He pulled on a clean t-shirt and went into the house looking for the kitchen.

The smell of freshly cooked food had already filled the room, and his hunger clawed at his stomach.

"People usually say '*good morning*' or at least '*hi*' when they see each other in the morning," he said in a conversational voice, leaning on the jamb of the door, his legs crossed at the ankles.

"Maybe they do, but I don't have time for niceties, especially with the likes of you," she threw over her shoulder with disdain, keeping busy at the stove.

"Oh, really? The likes of me? And what's so important that you can't pay the slightest courtesy to a guest?"

She made a grimace and thanked God he couldn't see her face. *'Courtesy, indeed! To a guest! As if I had invited him!'* Yet she didn't find an appropriate reply.

She should have worked for her next exhibit, but inspiration evaded her for the moment. She actually didn't have anything special to do. She'd already finished cleaning the ranch house.

Now, she thought of listening to some music, reading a book or simply admiring the nature. She'd find herself something to do and she didn't need him around.

"Things," she replied unfriendly, to close the subject.

"What kind of things?" he insisted, which prompted her to roll her eyes with exasperation.

He was like a terrier with a bone in his teeth. His jaw was stubbornly set and it was obvious he wouldn't let very well go.

"Various," she replied without showing any particular interest in him. "Not that it's your business, by the way."

She worried that if he hadn't left soon he would have driven her mad. Turning to him with the pan in her hand, she laid the omelet on his plate and snapped at him angrily, "Now, eat and leave!"

"Nice manners, really," he drawled his words without backing down.

Her rude treatment didn't seem to affect him. He looked as if he had the time of his life and she couldn't understand why.

"What's wrong with you?" she gave up and asked, watching the man with astonishment. "Don't you feel when you're not wanted somewhere?"

"Oh, yeah, I do, don't worry," he waved his hand. "It's not like you haven't gone out of your way to let me know you didn't want me here, sugar," he replied matter-of-factly. "Now, whether I want to or not, I have to stay here," he said, sitting down and forking some of the eggs she had prepared for him.

"What on Earth do you mean?" she asked him completely stunned.

She crossed her arms under her breasts and threw him a dark glance. She couldn't believe her ears. He had simply stated he had to stay there as if her wishes hadn't mattered at all.

"It's simple, sweetie pie. I have to stay here. Didn't your attorney read your aunt's will to you?"

His words left her speechless for a few seconds. She was just staring at him as if he'd suddenly sprung a new head.

"I didn't listen very attentively," she admitted in a mutter. "But I am pretty sure that I am the only one who inherited this house," she waved her hand around.

"Yeah, you are. But there's something else in there. She asked that you share the house with me for at least two years. That's the condition attached to your ownership. I'll take care of the property for two years, until you decide whether you really want to live here or not."

Her eyes grew so round that he was afraid they'd burst. The next moment, she rushed out of the kitchen and went noisily into the next room. A drawer was opened with nervous gestures.

A satisfied smile flourished on his lips at the sound of papers shuffled around. He knew he'd just stated the truth and wondered how she hadn't seen that condition before.

His reasons for being there were a bit more complicated than that, though. He couldn't care less about the state of the house or of the property.

He was there for her protection and to uncover some dark truths. Some people were long overdue a payback. The late old woman had just made it easier for him to find satisfaction when she wrote her will.

Those thoughts turned his smile into a sneer. There were things he couldn't forget or forgive. Payback was a given.

Her loud outraged shout and the sound of a drawer slamming in the other room prompted him to school his features into a mask of indifference. He resumed his eating with measured gestures.

She came back, mad as a hornet's nest, and leaned over him, "What the hell is this? Why is she doing this to me?"

"Doing? Sweetie pie, she's already done it," he replied quietly and continued eating his breakfast, unconcerned.

"You know what I mean," she stomped her foot. "Damn it, I'm too furious to think," she snapped and started to pace the length of the kitchen.

"Are you? Then, sit down and eat," he said, pushing the plate with eggs in front of her. "Maybe that will help your thinking process."

"I'm not in the mood to eat anymore," she snapped back. "Do you think I can eat when I know that a stranger is going to share the house with

me? And not any stranger, but you...,"
she sputtered.

"Why not?" he raised an eyebrow.
"You can't do anything about it, can
you? The will is extremely clear, if I'm
not wrong. It's ironclad. You can't
change a thing. And what's wrong with
me? Is there another man more suited
for this than me?"

She didn't bother to reply to him.
She looked for a way out, but she knew
very well that there wasn't any. The will
was clear and it wasn't as if she could
have changed it.

She glanced at him with a frown
between her eyebrows. She found
herself literally at his mercy.

That realization made another
thought pop into her head. She tilted her
head and watched him through her
lashes.

"What would it take to make you
leave here for good and leave me alone,
hmm?"

"I won't leave, so sit down and eat,"
he said, always calm, without emotion.

"Why not?"

She had almost shouted at him like a banshee, losing the thin shreds of control she had over her temper.

"Why can't you be a reasonable boy?" she asked meanly, and her eyes narrowed into thin slits.

He raised his eyebrows when he heard the appellative and his features turned sterner.

"Okay, a reasonable man, then," she said quickly, trying to appease him. She imagined he didn't care for her choice of words.

Yet, she knew she needed his consent after all, so perhaps it wouldn't do to alienate him.

"I'm reasonable. I'm reasonable because I don't intend to let the judge know of your pathetic attempt to make me leave. It sounded like a bribe, didn't it?"

"You are the worst -" she started but he stopped her with a brief gesture.

"I wouldn't continue if I were you. I've already finished eating. I'm going to wash my plate, so that you didn't have any reasons to complain that you are the only one doing any work around here," he mocked her, taking his plate to the sink.

She huffed behind him and because her temper was pricked again, she threw her fork to him, nailing him straight in the middle of his back. She'd already realized her childishness when he turned his head to her, his eyes as icy as a cold winter day.

Now, he turned completely to her and watched her for a long moment, as if he couldn't believe his eyes. He braced his hands on his hips and stared her down.

He'd thought she was just a pretty little thing. He hadn't imagined she'd have it in her to really get angry. Now, he realized how wrong he'd been and promised himself not to be so rush in his assumptions in the future.

He sighed and then, he asked quietly, tilting his head, "What the hell is wrong with you?"

"There's nothing wrong with me, beside you, of course," she replied and she crossed her arms over her chest. "I didn't ask for a housemate, did I, now?"

'You've got a point there, sweetie pie,' he thought. He reckoned she felt cheated and with her back to a wall, but he wasn't stupid to say it out loud. She'd have taken advantage of his understanding and he couldn't have any of that.

"Okay, sweetheart, let's settle this," he said and walked toward her with measured steps.

Her eyes sparkled with anger. She clearly didn't like to be called *'sweetheart'*. She bristled every time he used an endearment. He merely grinned at her and that fed her anger more.

"There's nothing to settle. You just have to leave. That's all!" she snapped and stomped her foot on the floor, at the same time.

'Way to go, girl. You're just regressing more and more,' she chided herself with derision.

"Now, you know I can't do that, don't you? I'd like to respect the old woman's last wishes. You should too. After all, she was your aunt, not mine," he replied with false sadness.

'*As if you cared,*' she tightened her teeth and scowled at him.

He knew she'd have liked to throw him as far away as possible, but unfortunately for her, he was there to stay.

He had some unfinished business to deal with and he didn't have any intention to let a pretty face get in his way. Yet, he commiserated with her because he understood how it was to feel powerless at the whims of fate.

"So, how do you see this situation?" she asked after a few moments of silence.

She pinned him with her narrowed eyes, while she was tapping her foot impatiently.

"As it is. I will live here for the next two years, whether you like it or not. You choose what bedroom I'll use. I'm not pretentious so I can sleep in any of them. Keep in mind, the barn is out of question." He put his hand up to forestall any replies. "My mother raised a gentleman, not a farm boy."

She snorted at his words and stared at him coldly. At first, she didn't make any effort to reply. Then, she couldn't keep her mouth shut anymore and said, "I doubt it."

"What?" he asked with a frown, although he had a good guess what she was talking about.

"I doubt the part where you're a gentleman," she said and headed to the kitchen door.

"Hey, you, where are you going?" he hurried after her, afraid she might think of running away. That would have put a serious hitch in his carefully laid plans. He needed her there.

"Hey, you?" she turned back to him with visible irritation. Suddenly, she felt so sick of his manner of talking to her that she felt like slapping him over the head.

"Till we make the introductions, sweetie pie, I'll call you that," he said coldly.

He felt a twinge of guilt because he had to trample all over her to reach his own goals, but he smothered it at once. The final goal mattered. What happened in the process of reaching it wasn't relevant at all.

Only then, she realized she didn't even know his name or where he came from. She knew nothing at all. She'd scanned over the words in the will and his name hadn't registered in her mind.

He was a stranger and she was supposed to share the house, and implicitly her life, with him. She doubted she'd be able to have a completely separate life with someone else in the house.

"Yes, we skipped that," she admitted morosely. "Our conversation was so titillating that we didn't find the time for introductions," she continued, sarcasm dripping off her tongue. Her eyes shone with scorn and something else, he couldn't put his finger on.

A grin claimed his lips. He was relieved that, at least, she had a sense of humor. Living with her might prove less boring than he'd expected.

"So, sweetheart, what's your name, then?" he asked leaning with his hip on the table. His arms were crossed on his chest, as if he'd wanted to keep her at bay.

"Diane and not sweetheart, so don't call me that anymore," she retorted with a scowl.

"Okay, not a problem for me, baby," he said, and his smile reached his eyes this time.

His lips twitched with pleasure when she clenched her fists at his new term of endearment.

"Damn it, man, I'm not your baby, is that clear?" she scolded him.

"Crystal clear, don't worry. I will try not to say it again," he replied, laughing now. "It's Adam to you," he said and bowed his head with ridicule.

"To me? Does that mean you have several names you use?" Diane asked him befuddled.

"It depends on the situation," he admitted. "Anyway, you have the honor to use the real one. Isn't that something?" he asked mockingly and a playful light danced in his dark pupils.

"Oh, stop doing me any favors. I can live without them," she snapped, stomping out of the room, her back straight as an arrow.

"I'm sure you can," he mumbled to himself as she was leaving the room.

CHAPTER 3

Adam decided to let Diane cool down for about half an hour and take care of his own problems. She'd been pretty riled up and he doubted she'd listen to reason.

He washed the dishes stacked in the sink, his mind mulling over the plans he'd already made and ticking the security measures, he had to take, off a mental checklist, one by one.

When he finished with the dishes, he brought his things from the barn into the house and left them in the kitchen until he had somewhere else to store them.

Adam intended to keep his part of the bargain and let Diane decide which bedroom he could take. She wasn't the enemy and he didn't want her to become one, even though he enjoyed nettling her all the time.

He knew that choosing a bedroom for him wouldn't have been a difficult decision to make. There were only three bedrooms in the house and she'd already moved into one. She had to decide if he'd take the one on the right or the one on the left.

The thought made him smile. Adam imagined that Diane regretted that she hadn't listened to that lawyer more carefully, now. If she had, she'd have known that company was about to come and she'd have chosen one of the other bedrooms, not the one in the middle.

He'd seen her in the window earlier when she was watching him and he'd guessed which room was hers. Her aunt had given him a tour of the house when they met a few months before her demise and he'd committed everything to memory.

Old habits always died hard. He'd been conditioned for several years to plot and memorize the layouts of the buildings where he had to live even for only a few hours. He doubted that would ever change. Caution was too ingrained in him.

He'd liked the old lady. Martha was the salt of the earth and he'd felt comfortable in her presence. She liked him as well, not like her niece, who seemed to abhor the ground he walked on.

He'd spent several weeks with her but he'd had to leave for a short while and put his affairs in order. When she died, he was far away. The lawyer informed him after the will was read and he felt as if he'd lost another family member.

Martha Elgin was another one to avenge. Her death had been ruled an accident, but he knew better. The timing of her death was telling.

Adam shook his head to get rid of his bleak thoughts. He needed to look forward not backward. He couldn't bring Martha back to life, but he could keep his word and take care of her niece.

Adam glanced at his watch and lifted an eyebrow. Diane had taken a lot of time to get over her anger and he didn't intend to give her a minute longer.

He went out into the hallway and yelled, "Diane, come downstairs. We have to talk things over. I don't have all day to wait for you."

His voice sounded harsh, but a smile appeared on his lips when a door slammed upstairs and Diane stomped down the stairs.

She stopped a few steps from the bottom and with one hand braced on her hip, she scowled at him.

"Who died and made you my boss?" she asked with fire in her voice.

He just arched his eyebrow again and refused to answer. Yet, a blush powdered Diane's high cheekbones when she realized the insensitivity of her words.

"All right, forget that. What do you want now?" she scolded him.

Diane disliked herself because she behaved like a teenager. Her maturity seemed a matter of the past. The man brought out the worst in her. She lost any measure of control when Adam spoke to her.

"First, a bedroom to leave my things and second, your car," he answered curtly and, without waiting for a response, he headed back into the kitchen to pick up his backpack and the cowboy hat, he'd left on a chair.

"My car?" Diane came after him in a rush. "Why would I give you my car?" she asked with befuddlement.

He ignored her question and picked up his things with lazy gestures. Only after he had everything secured in his hands, did he glance her way and deigned to answer to her.

"Because I need to go back to my car and take what I left in the trunk. I won't walk all those miles again," he replied mildly.

The distance didn't daunt him. In his former life, he'd marched longer than that and had even run over longer distances. Yet, he didn't feel like spending the day walking over five miles one way, then back again to bring the rest of his luggage.

He didn't have a lot of stuff but carrying a suitcase through the woods was far from his idea of having fun. Besides, he didn't want to be away from the ranch for too long.

Leaving Diane alone for longer stretches of time was out of question. He'd cursed himself enough when he found out she'd been alone there for the funeral. His worry and self-loathing had increased when he couldn't make it there immediately after she moved in.

"I'll drive you," she said and went to take the car keys from her bag.

"No need," he refused sternly. "I can drive myself there and back without problems. I've been driving since I was fourteen."

"Fourteen? That's-"

"Precocious, I know," Adam interrupted her with mirth.

He knew she'd wanted to say something else and smiled. His charming smile wormed its way right into her heart.

'No, not my heart. What the heck am I thinking? I don't find him anything but overbearing,' Diane thought.

She gave herself a mental shake, and said, "It doesn't matter. I won't let you drive my car. Either I drive or you can walk. You choose." She ended in a voice that didn't leave room to bargain.

'I thought she was an airy butterfly, but she seems to be a barracuda,' Adam reflected with puzzlement.

He didn't like it when he was wrong. Some mistakes didn't leave room for new ones.

Martha had told him Diane was an artist. Artists lived with their minds in the clouds, didn't they? They weren't supposed to be belligerent.

"All right, your *Stubbornness*," he said and bowed mockingly. "Lead the way," he continued with a large gesture, and left his things in the kitchen. "At least this way, we can try to start my car. I have some jumper cables in my trunk."

Diane looked at him with suspicion and Adam found that amusing. The woman proved to have no gullible bone in her body.

That put a stitch in his plans but, in the long run, he preferred it that way. At least, he wouldn't be bored to tears in no time at all.

Those last few years had made him indifferent to women. Probably because he'd met a certain type of woman all the time. He rarely turned them down, but one encounter was more than enough.

"I can show you to the car," she replied, "but you'll have to show me where your car broke down," Diane turned her back to him and headed out of the house.

CHAPTER 4

Adam watched Diane drive and admired her competence. She took every bend with precision, even though her speed was just a notch higher than people would normally try on those meandering mountain roads.

"What?" she asked, slightly turning her head to him for a second. "You're staring. Have I grown horns all of a sudden or what?" she snapped when she noticed Adam's annoying smile.

She was irritated all right. The man knew how to smile. Every time he turned that grin toward her, the butterflies in her belly started a hoopla dance and that was disconcerting. She couldn't wrap her head around that reaction at all. It was both new and unsettling.

Adam muddled her mind and she needed her wits to stand up to him. She had the feeling the man would trample all over her otherwise and that wasn't something she would abide.

"Just enjoying the view, pumpkin," he replied with a grin.

"Diane, not pumpkin, remember?" she barked at him again.

She had to set him straight. Every time he uttered one of those silly endearments, her silly heart forgot that it was just for show and beat faster.

'I suppose it's the accent or because he drawls his words,' she reflected. Yet, she knew that she was well over the age when such things should make her reason melt into a puddle.

Adam just shrugged with indifference and replied, "You know that old habits die hard, Diane. You're fresh and sweet enough, and that makes me call you pumpkin or sweetie pie."

Her eyes widened and bewildered, she looked at him for a moment, forgetting to watch the road. The car turned slightly to the right, where the mountain slope tilted toward a deep valley.

"Watch the dang road, woman," Adam shouted and immediately, she snapped out of her trance and righted the car.

"If you promise to watch the road, I'll promise not to call you pumpkin anymore, all right?" he said with obvious relief.

For a brief moment, he'd visualized the car flying into the abyss below and it unsettled his stomach. He hadn't survived bullets and bombs just to end up a statistic in a car accident.

"Or, if you prefer, I can drive myself, as I proposed from the beginning," he continued to mutter, although loud enough to be heard. "That way, I might get to my car alive."

"I can drive," she protested. "It was just a moment of distraction, that was all," she said defensively and a blush crept all over her cheekbones, neck and ears.

Diane hated it whenever she blundered something. In her book, there wasn't any room for mistakes. Her mother had drilled that into her head time and time again.

Her fingers clutched the steering wheel and she clenched her teeth. She'd have screeched in frustration, but didn't want to give him the satisfaction that he'd rattled her enough for that.

"One moment's more than enough," he replied heatedly. "Who the heck had the bright idea that women should drive? Who the heck decided to give them a driver's license?" he asked rhetorically, rolling his eyes and gesticulating widely.

"You're a chauvinistic pig," she observed, forgetting about her earlier mistake. "Women drive very well, even better than men, if you must know," she replied and increased the speed just to show him how wrong he was.

She'd never backed down from a dare and his words dared her big time. Diane knew her behavior was childish, yet, she couldn't control her reactions around him. She had to ponder about that.

"Hey, Diane, let's say I believe you. There's no need to kill me just trying to prove a point," he said in a conciliatory voice and patted her on the knee, which startled her.

His gesture shocked her and the car took another nose dive toward the edge of the road.

"Oh, God, woman," he groaned and tried to grab the steering wheel with his left hand.

She growled at him and steered the car back on the road, after she slapped his hand away. She pushed the gas pedal down some more.

His eyebrows shot up and not only because of her growl. He stared at her, speechless. Diane kept surprising him.

Once the road widened for a fraction, she brusquely pulled over on the shoulder of the road and turned off the engine. Her hands trembled on the wheel but not because of fear.

Diane was so angry that she barely controlled herself. She felt like hitting him over the head with a blunt object and she didn't like it.

She'd never thought of herself that way. She wasn't a violent person, but since his arrival in her back yard the night before, she'd gone through the wringer.

"Get out of my car, now," she said in a low and menacing voice.

Or what, pumpkin? Adam replied mutely, but decided to try a different path. He turned to her and watched her steadily.

The wisps of coppery hair framing her face tantalized him. His fingers itched with the need to push them away and touch her skin.

"What now?" he asked as if he hadn't understood what was going on.

"You've picked on me since the moment you arrived," she bellowed, forgetting everything about her own lecture about control and self-restraint. "I'm sick of your macho behavior and your misogynistic views. I'm sick of you, period. Now, out," she practically roared and her small hands clenched into fists and pounded the steering wheel.

She'd have preferred to pound his face, but she refused to lower herself to a physical attack. Plus, she didn't know how he would react and she was smart enough to guess that she wouldn't win in a contest of brute force.

"Yeah, as if..." he smirked at her. "Just because I pointed out your driving shortcomings," he shook his head. "Diane, Diane, it seems to me you don't take criticism too well, sweetheart, even when it's warranted. You can't say you weren't about to drive us down there twice." He pointed his thumb toward the slope of the mountain.

He glanced at the valley stretching at the bottom of the abyss and shuddered mentally.

"And it's not a gentle slope, you know," he thought to mention and glanced again toward the side of the mountain. *'Dang, it's a long way to the bottom of that valley,'* he noticed.

"Because of you, not because I can't drive, stupid," she replied hotly, and this time, she did slap his arm.

"Because of ol' me?" he asked with innocence, pointing his thumb to himself and beating his lashes with exaggeration.

"You know very well what you did," she replied with tiredness in her voice.

She braced herself and breathed deeply. She tapped her impatient foot on the floor of the car and, then, she repeated with calm, "Now, get out. You should be close to your car. I'll be home. Don't expect a warm meal when you come back," she continued and looked straight ahead. She refused to acknowledge what he might thought of her.

Adam noticed that she avoided looking at him and felt a perverse joy knowing he rattled her. That joy disappeared fast enough when he realized she was serious.

'The dang woman does expect me to walk to my broken car and back to the ranch,' he thought and decided to pay more attention to her from that moment on. Diane proved more difficult than he'd expected. He thought he'd handle her with ease.

"You can dream on, little girl," he snorted. "I'm not beyond grabbing you and throwing you in the back of the car, Diane," he said, his icy eyes trained on her.

Diane looked up sharply and shuddered when she met his look. Her eyes searched his face and she cringed. *'He's serious. He'll do it. Oh, Lord, what now?'*

"You're threatening me?" she chose to attack, even though her voice shook a little.

"If necessary, yeah. You should know something about me, pumpkin-"

"Ah!" she interrupted with another growl. "First of all, I told you not to call me pumpkin anymore," she started in force, but he put up his hand and stopped her.

"I said I wouldn't if you watched the road. Should I remind you, *pumpkin*, you didn't?" he observed, just to needle her some more.

Adam didn't understand his need to pick on her and drive her mad. '*Maybe because she drives me mad just because she breathes,*' he had a brief moment of honesty with himself, but buried it immediately.

He couldn't take that road. His priorities laid somewhere else. Besides, he didn't do steady relationships and Diane definitely didn't fall under the one-night-stand type.

"You touched my leg," she accused and her green eyes flashed at him.

"So what?" he replied nonplussed. "Has no man ever touched you?" he shrugged with nonchalance, as if his gesture hadn't been out of the ordinary.

And it wasn't, Diane admitted, but with him, it seemed different and she didn't like that different. She preferred relationships that didn't make her think too much. She liked polite men who understood to leave her alone when she wanted to be alone and didn't dare to take the initiative and order her around.

"Only when I said they could," she retorted with disdain. "I didn't give you permission to touch me," she specified in a haughty voice.

"Don't tell me you went out only with guys who asked nicely if they could touch your hand or kiss you," he exclaimed and looked at her in shock.

"Not that it's any of your business, but, as I said, I prefer polite men," she said and nodded with emphasis.

"I think you confuse polite with milquetoast, Diane. A considerate man would back off if you said no, but there's no way, no way in hell, a red-blooded man would ask permission for every touch," he shook his head.

"Whatever, get lost," she gave up. "Walk straight ahead and you'll find your car," she continued, waving to the road.

"You said *first of all*," Adam said as if she hadn't asked him to leave.

"So what?" She looked at him befuddled.

"That means you also have a *second of all*. Let's hear it," he proposed.

Adam had no intention of getting out of the car or losing sight of her. He planned to stay as close to her as possible for the following two years. If his plans needed two years to be completed.

Even if his constant presence nettled her, he had a job to do. Her wishes came second or even last, depending on the circumstances.

"I forgot what I wanted to say." She threw her hands into the air. "So, there you have it. Now, get out," she repeated meanly.

"I haven't," he replied. "I remember perfectly." He decided to enlighten her.

"I said *'You should know something about me, pumpkin'* and you replied, *'First of all, I told you not to call me pumpkin anymore.'* So, you do have a *second of all*," he ended with glee.

"Now I remember, thank you so much for reminding me," she replied sarcastically.

She crossed her arms under her breasts, which pushed them higher, and his eyes zeroed in on them in a nanosecond flat.

"I intended to tell you that what I know about you is enough. I don't need to hear anything else," she nodded with determination.

"Well, that's where you're wrong," Adam replied with a false compassionate voice, looking up at her face.

"What do you mean?" she asked, with a feeling of dread invading her body.

"You'll have enough time to find a lot out about me," he replied. "Well, not everything," he admitted. "I'm not an open book after all. And the first thing you'll find out is that I'm not a doormat, Diane," he specified, his eyes boring into hers. "You can't trample all over me and bring me to attention with a few choice words, pumpkin. I'm the boss, not like the men you've led on a leash so far," he said with authority and put his hand up again when he saw she wanted to interrupt him. "Don't bother. You can do whatever you want as long as it doesn't clash with what I want," he explained very matter-of-factly.

"You're out of your mind," she concluded and her eyes widened again. "Do you really believe you can order me around?"

"No," he shook his head, "I'm not thinking of ordering you around. I'm just stating how things are. What I say comes first," he said in a serious voice.

"In your dreams, big boy," Diane waved him off and rolled her eyes.

Suddenly, his demeanor changed. His eyes turned hard and he leaned toward her.

"I'll let that slide," Adam responded in a low voice, "because I know you don't know what I know. But listen well, Diane, and I'm darn serious about this, girl. You do what I say, for your own good."

"You threatened me again," she observed with amazement and shook her head. She couldn't believe his boldness.

"It's not a threat," he said and grabbed her arm, which startled her again.

A trace of fear appeared in her pupils and he didn't miss it. His heart cringed at the thought she believed that he'd hurt her.

"I don't want to scare you," he said in an even voice. "You needn't be afraid of me. I won't hurt you, Diane, but you need to listen to me from now on and listen well. Your aunt didn't put me in your proximity just to play a prank on you," he explained further. "She had a serious reason. You're a smart woman, from what I could gather. Think before doing anything unreasonable."

Diane just stared at him. His fingers burned her skin and his words shocked her.

"What do you mean?" she asked in a small voice.

He might not have wanted to frighten, her but he did that all the same.

"It's not the moment now. We'll rehash all that later." He shook his head. "You only need to know that my presence here is necessary and your cooperation is imperative," he decided to tell her.

"Oh, no, you don't," she snatched her arm away from him. "Either you tell me what's what or I do what I think I should do, what I please, and the heck with everything else," she said.

Stubbornness was written all over her face. Her green eyes sparkled with rebellion.

Adam sighed deeply and prayed for patience. He decided to end the stalemate and offer her an olive branch.

"Okay, you drive for the moment. Go on, I think we're close to the place where I left my car."

Diane wanted to insist, but noticed his weariness and that stopped her. She turned the key in the ignition and drove away, paying attention to the road so he wouldn't find yet another reason to cut her to ribbons with his words.

CHAPTER 5

Adam found his car exactly where he'd left it. With satisfaction, he noticed that no one had touched it.

He'd left telling signs and they hadn't been disturbed, with one exception. An animal had probably climbed onto the hood and fooled around with the windshield wiper, because, otherwise, if someone of the human variety had checked his car, the other signs he'd set up would have been disturbed as well.

Diane's eyes followed Adam's every move. After what he'd said in the car earlier, she decided to keep her eyes wide open. Something was going on and it was definitely something fishy.

She didn't know whether she could trust Adam or not. Her aunt had trusted him, though, and Diane knew Martha hadn't been anyone's sucker. She could sniffle a bad man better than any hound.

Curiosity lit the green of her pupils and her teeth bit into her lower lip in concentration. She rubbed her hands warily, while watching Adam's telling movements around the car.

Adam glanced at her. She amused him and at the same time, she touched his heart. He could read everything on her face and a smile fluttered on his lips.

"What are you doing?" she asked with impatience. She couldn't keep her curiosity in check anymore.

"Just making sure no one tempered with the car," Adam shrugged her question away.

After he answered to her, he crouched and checked underneath the car. Satisfied that no devices had been attached anywhere, he stood and said, "I have some battery cables in the trunk, as

I said. Do you think we could try to jumpstart my car?"

"Yes, of course. That way, you may leave me and my car alone," Diane replied maliciously. "It's not like we have to be joined at the hip all the time."

"Don't count on that," Adam replied in a quieter voice and opened his trunk.

He needn't look at her to know that his answer angered her. Her tension was palpable and enveloped him from everywhere. *As if I'd cared,* he thought.

He returned to the front of the car with a pair of jumper cables and found her in the same spot she was before. She hadn't moved from where he'd left her. A scowl etched on her features and she clenched her fists so hard her knuckles turned white.

"Why don't you lift your hood?" he inquired mildly.

Adam didn't want to alienate her completely because he needed her cooperation in the long run. Diane just speared him with her glare for a few more moments and then, she turned stiffly and headed to her car to lift the hood.

They worked in tandem for the following few minutes and their work was soon rewarded. Both Adam and Diane cheered when his engine started to purr.

They high-fived each other and laughed merrily together, for the first time, not at odds. Still on a peaceful ground, they started their trip back home, their differences put aside for the brief period they shared that small triumph. Neither of them lied to themselves. They knew their truce was temporary.

Diane parked behind his car and stopped the engine. She grabbed the keys and got out of the car, only to freeze with her hand on the car door.

Adam had already unloaded a suitcase from his trunk, but now he took out two rifles.

'What the heck does he do with a rifle? No, make that two. Is he a wacko with a penchant for guns?'

Adam glanced at her and grinned. He guessed what bothered her. As always, her face reflected her thoughts.

"It's close to hunting season," he explained the presence of the rifles with nonchalance.

'As if I knew what season it is. Huh! Although, I'm here for a hunt, so...'

"I don't know anything about any hunting season," Diane replied in a shaky voice, "but do you really need two rifles? And don't tell me you want to kill Bugs Bunny or Bambi," she shouted at him, regaining her gumption.

Adam rolled his eyes. 'Bugs Bunny? Bambi? What are you? Two years old?'

"Hadn't thought you'd still watch cartoons at your age. I'd have thought you were out of kindergarten." He shook his head. "I'd have brought you a Barbie if I'd known differently," he continued with biting sarcasm.

Diane bared her teeth at his words, which prompted him to laugh heartily. He did enjoy egging her on.

"Don't worry, I won't shoot Bugs Bunny, Daffy Duck or Bambi. I am trained for bigger game," he winked at her.

"I don't care what you're trained for," Diane snapped his head off. "You're a killer," she accused him with a frown.

"That, you got it right," Adam replied in a serious voice, and the light in his eyes died, which chilled her to the core.

He turned away and carried the suitcase and the guns into the house. Diane, riveted in place, looked after him, a dreary feeling creeping in her mind. The way he'd said those words didn't leave room to interpretation.

'I'm sharing my house and life with a killer,' she reflected and her hands shook. *'What were you thinking, Auntie?'*

Diane forced her feet to move and anxiously, she stopped next to Adam's

open trunk. She glanced inside the trunk
and her eyes bulged out.

CHAPTER 6

"What do you hunt with grenades?" she asked in a shaky voice.

Diane leaned on the jamb of the door to keep standing. When she'd seen the case with grenades aligned in their little holes like soldiers, she almost fainted. She'd seen grenades only in movies and that was some time ago, as she wasn't too fond of war films.

Adam slowly turned to her, his eyes two dark, unreadable pools. He tilted his head and his eyes swept over her body from the top of her head to the tip of her boots.

Adam's stance frightened her. The man looked like a panther ready to jump at her throat and sink his teeth in her jugular.

His latent strength and his secrets played havoc on her nerves and put forbidden thoughts in her head.

'You need to pull yourself together, girl,' she scolded herself. *'This is the type of man from which you have to steer far away. Forget about those biceps that made your mouth water in the morning.'*

Diane shook her head to get rid of her crazy thoughts and headed for the kitchen table where she let herself fall into a chair. She didn't think she could stand for another second.

The day hadn't spared her for one moment. She felt light-headed and she shook all over.

"That's for big game," Adam answered with nonchalance.

A grin appeared in the corner of his mouth, making him look like a rascal. Yet, his eyes were hard.

Diane was afraid to ask what he meant, but she needed to understand what was going on. He clearly hadn't come there just to annoy her.

"You have a freaking arsenal with you, Adam," she said and waved to the rifles he'd set on the kitchen table. "What, with two rifles and a case of grenades..." she continued.

"And to think you haven't seen it all," Adam replied softly and flexed his shoulders to work out some kinks in his muscles.

The last few days hadn't been easy on him. Sleeping in the barn the previous night didn't help him much, either.

"What do you mean?" she perked up.

She was sure he would get to the interesting stuff now.

"I mean I'm prepared for everything. What you saw is just the tip of the iceberg, Diane," he replied with a shrug.

"You mean to say that you have other weapons in your car?" she asked wide-eyed.

He nodded briefly and waited to see what else she was going to say or do. He didn't dare to guess her reactions any more. The woman had proved unpredictable enough.

"I see," she whispered and stared at him. "But why?" she asked. "Rarely wild animals come over here, you know. If you steer out of their path, they leave you alone. You don't need a… rifle or grenade for them," she explained patiently.

Adam laughed out loud. His laughter sounded ugly and hurt her ears. She winced visibly.

"What's so funny?" she asked, her shackles up.

"You, Diane, you're funny," he said and came to her.

Under her cautious eyes, he nudged the side of her jaw with his thumb. It felt rather like a caress and something jolted in her belly.

"Why?" she whispered, unable to speak.

"Because you make all these assumptions," he shrugged, and his thumb trailed the line of her jaw absently.

Then, he turned away and went back out to his car. Wide-eyed, Diane watched him leave.

She wanted to insist on getting real answers from him, but she felt rattled. She decided to wait for him there.

He returned with two duffel bags, one on each shoulder, and then picked up the suitcase he'd left near the table. He headed upstairs to the bedroom she'd assigned him.

Diane noticed he'd left the rifles behind. She eyed the guns with mistrust.

She'd always been a pacifist and she abhorred guns. She hated what people could do to other people using a weapon.

His jogging steps on the stairs pulled her back from her reveries. She glanced at the kitchen door. Adam came in and picked up one of the rifles, he'd left behind, and under her incredulous look, he stuffed it under the sink.

"What are you doing?" she shouted. She couldn't have stopped her words even if she'd wanted to.

"Prepping," he answered curtly to her, and grabbing the second rifle, he went into the hallway.

This time, Diane followed closely, just in time to see him conceal the rifle in the umbrella holder.

"Prepping for what?" she shouted exasperated, throwing her arms in the air. "Look, I'm sick of your ambiguous answers," she said. "I want the truth and I want it now," she continued and slapped the wall on her right.

Adam turned to her and pierced her with his look. He looked at her for something that felt like a long time and Diane started fidgeting under his unnerving gaze.

"You want the truth," he said softly. "All right, I'll give you the truth," he decided. "We can very well have some coffee with that, what do you think?" he said and strode back to the kitchen.

Adam didn't glance behind him. He knew she would follow him. He'd seen her curiosity. Her eyes had widened and her pupils had dilated.

"Have a seat," he invited her, but didn't turn to check if she followed his invitation.

Adam went to the coffee maker and filled the pot with water. He rummaged through a couple of cupboards until he found coffee and filters.

He prepared everything with measured gestures and didn't flinch once under Diane's sharp scrutiny, even though her eyes drilled holes into his back.

"Where's the sugar?" he asked her. "I suppose you take sugar in your coffee," he glanced at her, an eyebrow raised inquiringly.

"Not really," she shook her head. I prefer my coffee black and unsweetened."

"Good, me too," he said and finally, turned away from her. "You're almost out of coffee. We'll need to buy some," he observed and then, he opened the fridge.

Adam looked inside the fridge and visibly winced. He closed the door and turned to her.

"There are no eggs left, no bacon, just some weeds and a tomato," he accused. "What did you intend to do? Starve?"

Diane shrugged daintily and pretended she had some lint to pick up off her clothes.

Silence stretched for a few moments and then, she replied quietly, "I didn't count on you showing up."

Suddenly, she looked up at him with a deep frown. "Those aren't weeds. It's salad," she defended her food choices.

He scowled and braced his hands on his hips.

"Food for rabbits or ducks maybe, but definitely not for me. I can take a weed or two in my sandwich if everything else obliterates the taste, but otherwise...." he shook his head.

Diane smiled and observed with amusement, "I suppose you're a steak-type of guy."

"You got that right," he agreed with her assessment. "We'll have to go shopping," he decided on spot. He didn't feel like fasting until the following day.

"I won't go anywhere today," Diane refused, shaking her head. "I've had enough excitement for one day and I don't feel like going down to the town right now."

"I can't leave you here alone," he discounted her words in a hard voice that didn't broach any argument.

"I've been alone so far," she stubbornly said, unimpressed with the authority of his voice.

"Well, not anymore," Adam reiterated very matter-of-factly.

"No, I won't go shopping this afternoon," she replied in a stronger voice. "We're not joined at the hip, Adam. I might have to accept you in the house, but that doesn't mean that I will turn my life upside-down because of your dictates," she shook her head with vehemence, and her hair bounced full of life and stole his breath away.

Adam shook himself mentally and then, he took in her stubborn demeanor. As a reflex, he flexed his fingers, praying for patience.

"I see that I have to tell you the truth now," he concluded and rubbed the bridge of his nose.

Tiredness had crept on him unnoticed. He felt weary after the last few days, which he had spent crossing the country by car, with only three or four hours of sleep at night.

He had also been worried about what might have happened to Diane if he hadn't got there on time. Yet, he couldn't take a plane, not with the arsenal he needed with him. Leaving it behind would have amounted to the same result in the end.

On top of that, he had spent the previous night in Diane's barn after a five-mile march and a few-hour-long stake-out.

Sparring with Diane hadn't been an easy feat either, although that had spiced his day somewhat. The woman kept him on his toes all the time. Not that he really minded that.

"The truth would be good," Diane replied quietly when she noticed he had started woolgathering.

She had already waited for a couple of minutes, but Adam seemed lost in his own world, which didn't seem to be like him or, at least, like what she knew about him.

"What?" he asked absent-mindedly, rubbing his face with the tips of his fingers.

"The truth," Diane pointed out. "You said something about telling me the truth," she reminded him about the topic of discussion.

"Yes, I did," he nodded. "Just a sec, the coffee is ready," he put her off when the steam of the coffee maker penetrated his haze.

Adam filled two mugs to the rim and brought them to the table. He left one on the table before Diane and sat down in a chair across from her so he could have her under observation. He could observe her emotions from there.

"I'm here on a mission," he confessed to her, looking straight into her eyes. He wrapped his fingers around the mug and let the heat of the coffee sip into his skin. "Your aunt had been threatened a few times when she didn't agree to sell her land," he brusquely revealed.

Diane's eyes widened and her mouth opened in a mute *wow*.

"Close your mouth, sweetie pie," Adam said out of habit. "You wanted to know the truth, so that's what you get. But I don't want any hysterics or anything," he warned her in a hard voice, his eyes trained on her unnervingly.

"I'm not given to hysterics," she replied heatedly, her voice one note higher than normally, which belied her words.

'As if! My mother would have had my hide for a simple tantrum,' she scoffed.

"Good, then. Let me continue. A few of those threats materialized, but Martha still didn't agree to sell. She didn't like what those people wanted to do on her land and besides, I understand this ranch had been in her family for about five or six generations," he shrugged and sipped from his mug.

Diane nodded and she also took a mouthful of her coffee. She was parched and needed the strength of the coffee to hold her through his story.

Indeed, the ranch had been in their family for a long time. Her grandmother didn't want to have anything to do with it. She felt smothered there and wanted to make a life for herself in the city. She had hated the work on the ranch.

Aunt Martha had been the last one there. She had taken care of the cattle until she couldn't anymore.

As she had never married, she didn't have children to help her and a couple decades back, she stopped working the ranch. She sold the livestock and everything related to cattle breeding, and lived frugally from the benefits and her own vegetable garden. She rounded her income by renting land to her neighbors, but she had never accepted to sell.

"The last threat Martha received was a threat to her life. She knew that they would keep their word. However, she wanted to make sure you got the ranch and you were well taken care of. Then, she started looking for help and found me," he said pensively. "Or better said, we found each other," he almost whispered, musingly.

"How come?" she inquired in a nonplussed voice.

"There's no need to go into my personal life," he brushed her off, "but let's say that your aunt's enemies were mine as well. She knew I was determined to... take care of them and she needed someone like me to take care of you," he said in a no-nonsense voice and flipped his hand.

"You mean to say you're here for me?" she asked, and her cynicism showed not only in her voice. Her eyes lit with mistrust.

"Partly, yes. Mostly, I'm here because I have some payback to shovel and because I promised to Martha," he replied with a shrug, unconcerned with her mistrust, and then, he picked up his mug and drained his coffee.

He put the cup on the table, drummed his fingers on the tabletop for a few seconds and then asked, "How much time do you need to get ready to go into town?"

"I won't go into town," she replied and shook her head stubbornly. "I've told you I had enough today."

"You can't stay here alone," he retorted.

"The heck I can't. Just watch me," she said and, pushing her cup aside, she headed to the door.

"I can't leave you here by yourself," Adam stood up.

"Should I remind you that I was here by myself before you came?" Diane asked, turning to him. "Nothing will happen to me until you come back from town," she refused to back down. "I'm taking a nap," she announced him and left.

Adam felt uncomfortable leaving her alone. They needed food and coffee, but he needed much more to know she was safe.

"Will you promise to stay in your room?" he shouted, going after her.

"I'm not a child," she turned to him, a hand on the handrail.

"No, you're not," he muttered for his own ears. Of course, he'd noticed she was far from a child and that was the ban of his life. "It would be easier if you were," he replied loudly. "I could just ground you in your room. Diane, keep safe and stay inside. Don't go out until I come back. It's not a joke," his hard eyes held hers.

Diane just looked at him and then nodded. She turned around and jogged up the stairs, feeling his eyes glued on her back all the way up.

CHAPTER 7

Diane did try to sleep. She was exhausted, but her mind was restless and scattered all over the place. Adam's appearance and everything that followed had taken their toll on her.

She punched the pillow to make it more comfortable. It didn't work, though.

Diane willed her muscles to relax, using a relaxation technique, she'd learnt in one of her yoga classes.

Her eyes drifted to sleep and, with a soft sigh, she surrendered. Her muscles relaxed completely, yet her mind worked a double shift, filled with unsettling dreams.

After about an hour and a half, Diane woke up with a startle. Some noise had reached her ears, disturbing her fretful slumber. She slowly sat up and listened intently.

'*Yep, here we go again. Probably, the wind whipped the barn door,*' she thought and got out of bed, intending to go out and secure the screeching door.

Diane pulled her boots on and stood up. Only then, she hesitated. Adam had told her to stay put and not leave the house and she felt somewhat guilty for not listening to him.

'*He might have a point,*' she conceded and reflected some more. '*Nah, he just wants to scare me so that I didn't ask questions about him being here and his... personal things,*' she decided to dismiss his warnings and went out of the door.

Half way down the stairs, she stopped. '*What if he didn't lie?*'

She drummed her fingers on the bannister, reflecting on what he had said earlier.

'*No, his story was too outlandish. Too much cloak and dagger and all sorts of plots,'* she shook her head and started down again.

Diane went out of the house and paused on the veranda. Feet wide apart, her hands braced on her hips, she surveyed the yard.

The wind had picked up, indeed, and leaves danced all over the place. Fall came earlier in the mountains.

The barn door had been slammed against the wall and the wind kept swinging it. The hinge screeched every time the door moved and Diane cringed. She had to do something about that hinge. She couldn't stand it anymore,

'Well, not right now,' she thought. *'I'm not even sure what to use,'* she grimaced. *'Well, I'll see. For now, I'll just secure it and the wind won't move it anymore,'* she decided and headed to the barn with long strides. *'There must be some rope or something inside that barn,'* she decided.

Diane got to the barn and headed directly inside to look for a rope. She barely got inside the barn that she felt something move on her left and goose bumps broke on her skin. She dreaded what lurked in the shadow.

She turned to see what was there, but she didn't move fast enough. Something hit her over the head and she fell face down on the grimy floor of the barn.

'Adam was right after all,' she thought before she passed out.

When she came, her hands were already tide behind her back and someone was coiling a rope around her ankles. Her mind froze, any defensive thought flying out of the window.

She felt someone standing up over her and she kept her eyes shut, playing possum.

'Maybe they just leave me alone if they think I can't see or identify them,' she reasoned, yet her heart had already sunk into her boots. She had never been in such a dire situation and she didn't know what to do or how to react.

She couldn't see who was inside the barn with her, but she could feel their movement. There were at least two if not three people shuffling around. Their steps told her they had finally turned around and gotten out of the barn.

"My idea paid off," one of them said on their way out.

"Yeah, yeah, yeah," another replied bitterly. "We know, you've already said it twice," he chided.

The barn door shut after them with a bang. The sound of a latch falling into place reached Diane's ears and her eyes opened wide. Horror marred her features. It didn't sound too good for her.

The men were still talking outside and their voices still reached her.

"So what," the first one puffed. "I was right when I said we should wait down the road and see which one of them would leave. And now, we're finishing her off and have a convenient scapegoat. They'll think that guy did it. We got rid of both of them in one single move and that thanks to me," he gloated.

Diane had the wrenching feeling they were talking about Adam. *'They want him to be the scapegoat, but for what?'* she wondered at a loss of ideas.

But then the answer came unexpectedly. Her nostrils flared at the gasoline smell. She heard the gasoline splashing against the wooden walls of the barn.

Scared, out of her mind, she desperately looked around for some means to escape.

The barn was mostly dark. A sliver of light came through between two panels of wood where time and the elements had eroded the wood. Not that it helped much.

Nothing could help her, short of a miracle. She shook and the rope coiled around her wrists and ankles bit into her flesh. She was so terrified that her belly churned with a wrenching feeling. Tears ran down her cheeks, washing off the dirt, and stinging her skin with their salt.

Diane made an effort to keep her wits about her, not to give in to her terror. She needed something to cut through her binds and fast because she was almost out of time.

Then, time ran out and she cried out. The crackling of flames engulfed the barn. Her heart skipped a beat or two and she bit her bottom lip, frantically looking around for anything she could use.

The tongues of the raising flames helped her see more of the interior of the barn.

'Not that flames are a good thing, Diane. Oh, God, I'm losing my mind. I have to do something, and now,' she thought, eyeing the flames licking the ground her way.

Tears flooded her eyes and helplessness strangled her. Her fingers shook and she bit her lower lip again.

CHAPTER 8

Adam saw the flames through the trees lining the road and roared his anguish. His foot floored the gas pedal.

He didn't care about the sharp bends of the road anymore. Losing Diane meant a new failure and probably, one he couldn't live with.

Handling the steering wheel with his left hand, he rummaged through the glove compartment and took a revolver out. He laid it on the passenger seat without taking his eyes from the road or the flames painting the sky reddish. He leaned forward, and also took out the gun he had stuffed at the small of his back. He left it on his thigh, handy if necessary.

In less than three minutes, Adam reached the ranch yard and slammed his brakes hard, at a distance from the barn. He remembered he still had the grenades in his trunk and he was confident that they didn't need a bigger bonfire.

Adam didn't bother to turn the engine off. He just jumped out of the car, both guns in his hands, and ran toward the barn.

The flames had already engulfed the entire wooden building. The sound of wooden boards falling inside the barn brought a hideous scowl on his face.

With one second to think, he threw himself through the burning door and landed on the dirty floor, next to Diane. Flames licked at her, and her pants had caught fire.

Adam left the guns next to her and indifferent to the flames reaching for him, he patted down the flames on her pants with his palms.

The air smelt of burnt hair and he noticed the fire had singed a few of

Diane's locks. The burning bite of a flame on his back jarred him into action.

Adam stuffed his guns into his waistband and gathered Diane up in his arms.

By now, both of them had been coughing in earnest. Their eyes had teared up because of the smoke and they could barely see around.

He crouched with her cradled in his arms and surveyed their surroundings.

'We get singed no matter what way I choose,' he thought. *'I'll have to move fast, at least to help her survive.'*

Adam stood, always bent over the woman in his arms, and then made a run to where the barn door had been. Flames licked at his shoulders and hair and kissed his pants, but he didn't pay attention to the pain. He pushed ahead.

Once he cleared the building, his lungs burning, he ran to the pump. A blanket would have worked better, but he didn't think he could take the time and go inside for one.

He gently settled Diane down near the pump and quickly filled the bucket with water from down the old well and pulled it up.

'*I could have put her under the pump directly,*' he thought and shook his head. The idea had already come too late.

He threw the water from the bucket over her head and upper side of her body and she jerked.

A cry of indignation followed. Staggering, she tried to stand up, and pushed hard with one hand on the stone wall of the well.

"Calm down, Diane, don't move, just take your time," Adam said softly, and gently pushed her back down.

Diane looked up at him with red eyes and he winced seeing the traces of her ordeal on her face.

"Everything will be fine, sweetie pie," he whispered, "don't worry now."

He gently brushed his fingers over her stricken cheek.

Diane tried to focus her eyes on him and suddenly, her eyes bulged out and she shouted, "You're on fire, you... stupid."

She tried to stand up again while he took stock of the flames biting their way through his pants.

Adam pushed her back down and she started patting his legs, to smother the flames.

He looked at her as if she'd lost it, and then lowered the bucket back into the well.

'Good going, man, he thought. *'You've lost your fucking mind for a broad and forgot about your well-being,'* he shook his head with disdain.

'Who'd take care of her if you went up in flames? Luckily these pants won't let the flames go through.'

He pulled the bucket out of the well and splashed it over his head. Then, he stretched his legs, one after another, under the pump and let the cold mountain water take care of the remnant flames.

He knew he had a few burns on his back, arms and legs. It hurt badly, but at least, they both were alive.

"Thank God, you came back when you did," Diane whispered barely audible.

She'd prayed for a miracle when she couldn't untie herself and her efforts to crawl to safety didn't have any results. Adam turned out to be her miracle.

Adam's eyes checked her all over. She seemed all right. Yet, he couldn't discount the effect the fire had had on her lungs and airways. He knew he had to have her checked out in a hospital.

He pulled her up and said, "I'll take you to the hospital in a few minutes. On the way there, you can explain to me why I found you in the barn when I asked you not to leave the house."

At his hardened expression, her eyes widened and her hand shook. Diane hadn't recovered completely and she wasn't sure she could withstand him.

"Now, where can I find a hose to douse this fire down? We can't risk having the entire forest go up in flames," he explained.

With a shaky finger, she showed to Adam where Martha had kept the hose for fighting fires. Her great aunt had also had a hydrant installed so a fire wouldn't extend to the neighboring areas. With so much wooden area around, fires weren't taken lightly.

CHAPTER 9

Adam put her in his car and strapped her in with the safety belt. He flexed his shoulders to work the kinks out of them. He had a new respect for firemen. It wasn't such an easy job to douse a fire. He felt scorched to the bones. Sweat dripped on his face and along his spine. He wiped off his face with a forearm, not paying any attention to the black streaks which marred his skin.

He went around the hood to get into the car when he remembered the food he had left inside the trunk.

'Damn, some of it will spoil until we're back,' he thought.

"If I leave you here in the car for a few minutes, can I hope to find you in the same spot?" he asked her, leaning inside the car.

Diane nodded, even though she didn't like how he constantly reminded her that she'd left the house.

Adam stared at her for a few moments and then, he took one of his guns out of his waistband and pushed it to her.

"If you need it, point it to the threat and just press this here," he told her, his finger indicating the trigger.

"I... I can't shoot someone," she stammered.

"Of course, you can," he nodded confidently and pushed the gun on her. "When your life is at stake, you can, trust me. Now, I'm going to unload the trunk and put a couple of things in the fridge. Keep your eyes open and do what I said if you're in danger," he repeated and slammed the driver's door shut.

The drive down the mountain was quiet. The silence was weighing down on her and the frown between Adam's brows never left his face.

Diane had been watching him since he came into the car after he finished unloading the groceries. Adam rarely spared a look at her. She couldn't read what was going on in his mind and it bothered her.

He drove down the mountain as fast as he dared and the car jolted her whenever he took a sharp bend.

"Adam," she said, at the same time grabbing at the handle above her window.

Adam had negotiated another hairpin bend and thrown her into the door.

"I think you can slow down," she tried to speak again.

The first time, she'd bit her tongue and she still tasted the metallic flavor of her own blood against her tongue.

"No, Diane, I can't slow down," he growled, baring his teeth. "Smoke inhalation is no joke, and God knows how much you had inhaled before I came."

Despite his display of anger, he used the same tone someone would use to talk to a child and she gritted her teeth in frustration.

"Probably, not so much," she said through her clenched teeth. "I'd have been burnt alive if you'd been five minutes late."

He shook his head in denial, although her account seemed accurate. Yet, he didn't want her to go down that road right then.

"But no car came out of the ranch. I don't believe they'd come on foot," he bit out.

"Probably, they took the trail behind the house. It leads somewhere down the road," she said and waved her hand in that direction. "Yeah, right there, do you see it?" she pointed to an opening masked by two big trees.

He glanced at the trail and swore a bleak streak. His fist hit the steering wheel repeatedly and made Diane wince.

When he visited Martha, he hadn't thought of verifying the trails. He'd imagined he'd have enough time to do it later.

Diane looked at him with wide eyes. Her fingers trembled on the handle she was holding with all her might.

Adam's face had darkened, his eyes threw spears and the diversity of his curse vocabulary surpassed anything she'd ever heard before.

She'd never witnessed anything remotely close to Adam's fury. She just hoped he wouldn't remember about her leaving the house again. She could live just fine without having that raw anger directed to her.

After a few minutes of raging against himself, Adam quieted. He glanced at her and took in the fear and fascination in her eyes.

'I frightened her,' he noticed with self-disgust and grimaced. Her fingers

shook on the handle and his guilt deepened.

Adam slowed the car down a notch and took her other hand in his. Lifting it to his mouth, he pressed a tender kiss on her shaky fingers and squeezed them.

"Diane, I might get angry at times and I might bellow and swear... Never, but never, fear I'd hurt you in anger," he stressed out and looked directly into her eyes. "I might lash out verbally, now and then, but nothing more. You're in no danger with me, okay?"

She faintly blushed and nodded. His lips on her fingers had done strange things to those butterflies who had taken permanent residence in her belly since his arrival.

"Now that I'm calm, can you explain to me why I found you in the barn, in the middle of that inferno, when I specifically told you to wait inside?"

He squeezed her fingers again to encourage her to talk and then freed her hand.

"Was it to goad me?" Adam asked again.

"Of course, not," Diane rushed to explain. "I just heard a noise and…"

"And you said, '*What the heck, let me go investigate. That Adam's so stupid he can't find his ass with both his hands so what if he said not to go out? What he says doesn't matter,*'" he snapped at her.

"If you continue to talk to me like that, I won't say another word," she threatened and frowned at him.

"Oh, yeah, you will," he said and sped up a little more.

The road had widened now and he could see the top of the rooftops in the valley.

"No, I won't. I won't be the subject of your ridicule," she tapped her foot on the car floor with determination.

"No, of course not," Adam said mockingly with a wide gesture. "As if it hadn't been ridiculous enough to go out to investigate a noise after someone had already explained the danger to you. Just like in a bad horror movie, Diane," he said and glanced at her with a frown. "You know what I'm talking about. The girl knows the guy with the axe is out there and she'd be safe inside but, no, she has to go out and get herself killed," he finished in a roar. "How smart is that? Now tell me, how smart is that?"

Adam glanced at her again and saw the tears running down her face. Guilt squeezed his heart again and he shook his head.

"All right, I'm sorry," he apologized.

'Why the heck I have to apologize is beyond me but I can't have her crying.'

Diane wiped her tears off with a nervous gesture and looked away from him.

"Diane," he called her softly but she didn't turn to him.

Adam chose to make her react otherwise and put his hand on her thigh. She practically jumped up.

"What are you doing?" she asked breathlessly, her eyes riveted on the big dark hand resting on her thigh.

"Just begging for your attention," he replied softly and grinned at her ruthlessly.

He squeezed her thigh and she flinched under his fingers.

"Are you afraid of me or does my touch disgust you?" he asked, his voices mildly curious, although his thoughts were far from mild. He waited her answer with dread.

"None of the above," Diane swallowed hard and replied in a small voice. "I was just... startled. I... didn't expect that and... Anyway, it's all right," she tried to put an end to her stammering, sick with her weakness whenever he touched her.

"Now, can you tell me what happened?" Adam asked again. "Right after you tell me where the hospital might be because I really don't know," he winked at her.

Diane felt a laughter erupting from her throat and she felt better than she'd felt all day.

Adam was unbelievable. He was outrageous and cynical and protective.

She had moments when she wanted to smother him in his sleep. Yet, there were moments like this that made her feel terribly alive.

CHAPTER 10

The visit at the hospital wasn't very funny. Adam hovered all over her and refused any kind of medical assistance for himself.

Diane made him accept to be checked out by the doctor when she informed him she would follow suit and wouldn't let the doctor examine her either.

Adam begrudgingly submitted himself to the doctor's checkup, although he knew he hadn't been severely hurt. Yet, he had promised her he would, and he didn't take a promise lightly.

He wanted her lungs checked out and all her scrapes tended to, so he relented. He demanded a CAT scan as well when he found out that she'd been hit from behind.

Right after he laid his eyes on them, the doctor insisted on calling the police. Adam didn't care one way or another, so he just shrugged.

The sheriff came and left, shaking his head in disbelief. As there was nothing left of the barn and the thugs had used gasoline, he didn't think a trip to the ranch would help, but he had to check the fire though.

He didn't believe he'd find any traces leading to the guilty party, but he had a job to do. Not doing his job meant to lose in the next election.

Adam shared the sheriff's opinion and promised to take care of Diane himself.

The sheriff had suspected him in the beginning. Diane had clarified everything when she divulged the discussion those men had after they tied her up. She might have suspected Adam as well if she hadn't witnessed their exchange of words.

The trip back to the ranch was mostly silent because both were exhausted. Dusk reminded them of the full day they had gone through and they felt tired to the bones.

Adam drove steadily now. He didn't rush. He knew the ranch wouldn't go anywhere and he still had to make a tour of the property when they arrived there. He needed to make sure no surprises waited for them. He took his time and cruised at forty miles an hour.

Besides, he wanted to give the sheriff enough time to finish his investigation, not that he expected any results out of that.

Suddenly, the ringing of a phone pierced the silence and Diane practically jumped out of her seat. The silence had been so deep before that she didn't expect it. Adam just glanced at her and smiled.

He leaned over her and took the phone out of the glove compartment. He checked the display first and then answered, putting the phone on speaker to keep his hands free for driving.

"Hey, Ryan. You're on speaker. What's up?"

"Just checking in. Everything okay?"

"Hmm. Why do you ask?" Adam replied and a frown formed between his brows.

"You know Kate," Ryan said apologetically. "She kept badgering me that something was wrong with you and... Kate, don't you dare hit me with that spoon again," he bellowed.

Adam laughed. "Spoon, Ryan?"

"Yes, she's making spaghetti and hit me with a big wooden spoon, so don't laugh. It's not funny."

"Poor, little baby," Adam crooned and Ryan swore.

"If he can ridicule me, he's fine," Adam heard him telling Kate. "You're fine, right?" Ryan asked again.

"Now, yes, I am," Adam confirmed. It felt good to hear his friend's voice.

"What do you mean, now?" Ryan's hard voice reached Diane's ears.

"We've had... let's say, a lot of lively moments around here today," Adam disclosed.

"Here being where?"

"Told you I was heading out to Montana," Adam reminded him. "Showed you on the map..."

"Right, you did. What happened? I can't believe Kate was right. Yeah, yeah, yeah, you were right, don't hit me again."

Adam laughed again. "I didn't know Kate had premonitions or visions or whatever they call that."

"No, she doesn't," a melodic low voice came through the phone, and Diane imagined it was that Kate they were talking about. "I just felt something was wrong with you and you needed help."

"Thanks, sweetheart," Adam replied. "I managed."

"But do you need help?" Ryan inquired. "Fess up, mate. Once a team, always a team. We always help each other, Adam," Ryan stated seriously.

Adam knew Ryan would react like that but he had been determined to solve that matter by himself. He glanced at Diane and her huge green eyes tugged at his heart.

"I might, mate," he replied without too much conviction.

"All right then. Nick will be there before me," Ryan told him. "He's in Montana after all, even though on the other side of Montana. I have to come from Montreal so it might take me twenty-four or forty-eight hours. I don't know yet," Ryan explained.

"I'll go with you," Kate said.

"No, you won't," Ryan replied in a hard voice.

"See that I will," Kate repeated very matter-of-factly.

Her stubbornness brought a grin on Adam's lips. He knew Kate well enough and he also knew that Ryan didn't stand a chance. Adam shook his head with amusement.

"We'll talk about that later," Ryan tried to detour the conversation.

"There's nothing to talk about. I'm coming with you and that's it," Kate didn't concede to his opinion.

"Damn woman," Ryan started to say and then, Adam and Diane heard, "Ouch! What the heck, Kate, you hit me over the head with that freaking spoon again!"

Adam burst out into laughter.

"Oh, man, you're done," he told Ryan.

"Yeah, yeah, yeah," Ryan replied. "Your turn will come, no worries. See you soon, buddy," he said and rang off, stealing Adam's chance to reply.

Adam shook his head with amusement and handed his phone to Diane.

"Could you put it back in the glove compartment?"

Diane took the phone and asked, "Who are Ryan and Kate?"

"A married couple," Adam chuckled and mischief shone in his eyes.

"And what's so funny about them being married?" she asked. Her voice showed she was cross.

"They're funny. They're perfect for each other," Adam specified and glanced at Diane. "Kate shovels a lot of things at him and Ryan is almost tame around her."

"Ryan's coming here to help you, isn't he?"

"Well, if I could have trusted someone to stay put when I said so, I wouldn't have needed him," Adam said and looked pointedly at her.

Diane blushed violently and waved her hand, "Are you going to hold that over my head for eternity?"

Adam seemed to think a few seconds about it and then said, "Yeah, I think so."

Diane's mouth opened in a perfect 'o'.

"You're ridiculous," she said with bewilderment.

"No, I'm not. I'm not the one going out to the barn to check on an open door after I was told not to leave the house," he pointed out in a steely voice.

"For God's sake, it was windy. I thought the wind opened the door and I just wanted to close it. The hinges are rusty and the door screeches at every move," she replied with exasperation.

"Nope, not anymore," he observed in a pragmatic tone of voice. "At least we don't have to worry about those hinges anymore," he shook his head.

Diane clenched her fists. *'Self-righteous prick,'* she thought, and the urge to hit him made her boil.

"Who's Nick?" she asked to change the subject.

"A friend."

"I presumed that," she said with frustration. "As Ryan is a friend. But what kind of friends?" she insisted.

"The best kind," Adam answered.

"Argh..."

Adam just grinned and continued to drive. Diane tapped her foot on the floor nervously.

"Hold your horses, sweetie pie. I'll tell you everything at home tonight," he promised and patted her knee.

Surprisingly, she didn't flinch. '*Hmm, that opens new possibilities,*' Adam thought and his brows shot up.

"I remember I told you not to call me sweetie pie," Diane observed, still cross with him.

"And I remember to have asked you to stay in the house, which you didn't," he retorted, and she growled impotently.

On the other side of the mountain, a grey-haired man threw his cell phone on the coffee table next to him and roared.

Blind with fury, he threw the glass with bourbon he had in the other hand. The glass shattered against the grill protecting the fireplace.

Panting with frustration, he stood up and went limping to the window. He'd hurt his leg while riding the week before, and his slightly overweight figure didn't help the healing too much.

He looked out the window for a few moments, then returned and grabbed the phone. He punched a number with shaky fingers. His fury raged in force.

"Mr. Phelps, good evening," he was greeted.

"Monroe," he said curtly. "How did your little task go?"

"We got her good, sir," the man snickered. "We tied her up in the barn and started a fire. The guy who was living there with her will get the blame."

"Are you sure?" Phelps asked through tightened teeth.

"Yes, sir," Monroe answered, but with less conviction than before.

Phelps's tone didn't announce anything good. It wasn't as if he hadn't known his boss's tone of voice.

"Did you make sure she was dead?"

"She couldn't have survived, sir," Monroe replied. "You should have seen the blaze…"

"You idiot," Phelps bellowed. "She's fine and dandy."

"It isn't possible, sir," Monroe replied with apparent conviction, but fear still rang in his voice.

"It is possible," Phelps retorted. "My driver saw her in the hospital. She wasn't even seriously hurt, you, imbecile. If you're not able to finish the job, I'll find someone else. You have a week," he ordered and rang off.

'No, I won't give him a week. Not even a day.'

CHAPTER 11

Adam checked the perimeter and, despite his exhaustion, laid out warning alarms all over the yard and at each possible entrance in the house. He knew motion sensors would be useless out there, with all the wild animals on the loose.

His eyes swept over the yellow tape the sheriff had put around the area where the barn had stood, and shook his head. It was just dust in the eyes.

Confident enough that they would enjoy a good night of sleep, which they both needed, he came back to the kitchen. The aroma of homemade food watered his mouth.

Diane kept busy in front of the stove. She looked adorable barefoot, her hips moving slightly while she stirred something in a pan. As if she had felt his presence, she turned and smiled at him.

His eyes swept over her heated rosy face. A few wisps of hair flirted with her skin. She blew them away and with a wave of her hand, invited him to seat down.

"I'll bring out the food now," she told him and turned the heat off. "Have a seat."

Adam sat down and his eyes followed her every move. He couldn't look anywhere else. He was bewitched.

She grabbed a couple of plates from the cupboard, together with two forks and knives, and laid them on the kitchen table.

"Need help?" he asked, ready to stand and join her.

"No," she patted his shoulder. "Just sit there and I'll be just a moment," she reassured him.

She went back to take the bread she had warmed in the oven. She had stuffed it with garlic and olives, and peppered it with Parmesan.

On her way back, she also grabbed two bowls with salad and brought everything back to the table.

"It smells fantastic," Adam smiled at her.

Then his eyes fell on the salads and grimaced. Diane just laughed.

"You won't die if you eat some salad," she reassured him, patting his shoulder. "You'll also have meat, don't worry. You won't starve."

"I didn't think I would," he mumbled, but she heard him and smiled.

When she returned with the stir-fry, he breathed easier. For a moment there, he had been afraid she went overboard to punish him and make him feel bad, and she cooked only vegetables.

They shared the meal seasoned with small chit-chat. When they finished eating and she brought the mugs filled with hot chocolate to the table, a feeling of contentment filled him.

"So, about Ryan and Nick," she said.

Adam grimaced, not very comfortable with the subject. He had forgotten she wanted to know about them.

"Is it a secret?" she asked, noticing his discomfort.

"No, not really… Or not anymore," he shook his head. "We worked together. A sort of spec ops team, if you want," he replied and looked straight at her. "When you said I was a killer, you were dead on."

"I didn't mean it that way," she rushed to say. "I thought you wanted to kill some defenseless animals."

He shrugged but didn't point out that some of the animals out there were anything but defenseless. Even for a man with a rifle, some were lethal.

"Anyway, I did kill, when the mission asked for that. I didn't kill for fun but that doesn't make me less of a killer," he explained in a very matter-of-fact tone of voice.

"I understand the difference," she protested.

"I doubt it," Adam replied drily. "You're a pacifist, remember? You abhor guns."

"As a norm, yes. But I understand that a man has to protect himself in a war or in missions like the ones you're talking about," she counteracted.

"Well, sometimes the mission was to kill so…" he said with nonchalance and then, he studied her to see how she took that.

Diane paled and her non-violent nature warred with his words. Yet, she knew that nothing was white or black and grey existed more often than people thought.

She met his studying gaze and tilted her head. Something occurred to her then.

"You want to shock me," she concluded and nodded.

"Yep," he admitted without any qualms. "Does it work?"

"Why would you want to do that?" she wondered, nonplussed.

"I want you to understand the type of man I am and what I'm capable of," he said, then braced his elbows on the table and leaned his chin on his fists, his eyes always trained on her.

"I doubt that killing defines you entirely," Diane replied softly.

"No, it doesn't," he conceded. "But I'm more than capable of doing it, and you can be confident I'd kill anyone who'd touch you."

That shocked Diane more than anything he'd said before.

"I don't want to bear that responsibility," she shook her head. "I don't want anyone dead because of me."

"Not even the men who tied you in the barn and set you on fire?" he inquired with disbelief.

She shook her head again.

"Are you serious?" he asked. "I bet those men are the ones who killed your aunt, too, Diane," he pointed out.

"I want them punished," she admitted. "Locked away so they couldn't harm anyone anymore," she replied in a small voice. "I don't think I want them killed."

"Listen to me and listen good," Adam stood up and leaned over her. His voice was hard and unyielding. "You won't interfere and get yourself killed in the process. You'll let me do what I have to do. Is it clear?" he thundered and his eyes shone with ice.

Diane nodded. She wasn't stupid and she knew she could get *him* killed if she interfered. That was the last thing she wanted.

Adam was a continuous pain in the neck but that didn't mean she wanted his demise. Quite the opposite.

She had to be honest with herself. The rogue attracted her and a lot. She'd never felt such a pull from any other man before.

Adam stared at her, trying to make sure she didn't just try to placate him. Satisfied with what he read on her face and in her eyes, he sat down again and drank half of his hot chocolate in one go.

Diane opened her mouth to ask something else when his cell phone rang again.

Adam put up his hand to signal her to wait and took the cell phone out of his pocket. He checked the name on the display and answered.

"Hey, Nick, how's it going?"

"You sound well enough," Nick's voice boomed out of the phone. "I'm on speaker," Nick noticed.

"Yeah, it seems I touched the darn screen again," Adam muttered. "Anyway, what's up?" he asked and laid the phone on the table.

"I'm on my way there," Nick informed him. "I was lucky to find someone to take care of my horses starting with tonight. I've been on the road for over half an hour. I'll get there before midnight. Is that fine?"

"Yeah, perfect. Just let me know before you drive into the yard. I set up a few booby traps," Adam explained.

"Nothing less than I expected," Nick observed.

"All right, I'll wait up," Adam said and disconnected the call.

Diane looked at him and her big eyes reflected her befuddlement.

"You're not very polite."

Adam just shrugged and stood up. He flexed his shoulder muscles in a move that seemed to be an ingrained habit to him. Diane couldn't stop herself to admire his physique.

"You work out," she observed and then blushed deeply when she realized she spoke aloud.

Adam just grinned at her and nodded. "Yes, it came with the job and now it's a habit. You like the results, don't you?" he winked at her.

Diane stunned him when she nodded her agreement. He had expected another potshot at him.

"We can give Nick the third bedroom," she observed to change the subject. "What about Ryan and Kate?"

"I'll give them my room and sleep on the sofa," he replied and pointed his thumb to the living room.

"I can sleep on the sofa," she remarked. "I'm smaller and I'll fit better there."

"No," Adam said.

Diane waited for a moment but he didn't comment anymore.

"Just no?"

"Yes, just no. You want explanations, I see," he said with resignation and brushed his fingers through his hair.

"All right, then. I can't leave you here downstairs alone. You'd be the first in the line of fire. And anyway, one must be here on guard so it can be me," he pointed out.

"But you won't be able to rest," Diane observed and picked up the two mugs to bring them to the sink.

Adam shrugged again and left the kitchen to verify the windows one more time. Diane shook her head after him and decided to wash the dishes.

CHAPTER 12

Nick arrived half an hour before midnight. Adam directed him through his booby traps and Nick managed to go through them unscathed.

Behind Adam, Diane watched the men bumping fists, tapping one another on the shoulders and then sharing a manly hug, without shame.

A smile fluttered on her lips when she noticed how strong their connection was.

Nick's eyes stopped on her and Adam took her hand and pulled her near him.

"Diane, this is Nick. Nick – Diane," he made the introductions, but he didn't let go of her hand.

Nick noticed and smirked at him. Adam felt awkward, but didn't care too much. He preferred feeling awkward than having Diane falling head over heels with his friend.

Nick looked like a bear, but Adam knew women had always found him very sexy. He didn't want to test that theory with Diane.

He didn't like the taste of jealousy. *'I don't even know why I'd be jealous. It's not like she belongs to me.'*

"Come inside," Diane invited him. "Adam will show you to your room and I'll make something for you to eat."

"You don't have to trouble yourself," Nick waved her offer away. "I can have some biscuits or…"

"No trouble at all," she smiled at him.

"How come you never smile at me like that?" Adam asked without thinking.

'I should sew my mouth, darn it,' he thought. He had the intense urge to club himself over the head.

Nick burst out into laughter and Diane blushed.

"What do you mean?" she asked him.

"Doesn't matter," he said and passed by her in a hurry.

"I think it matters," she replied and grabbed his arm.

Adam looked at her small hand on his arm and then looked up into her eyes. Diane really seemed concerned.

"With pleasure. Carefree… I don't know. But I know you've never smiled at me like that," he answered. He didn't make any effort to pull his arm away either.

"Probably because you needle me all the time," Diane replied. "Yes, I think that's it. You make me so angry all the time that I can't smile at you that way," she nodded.

"Well, I have reasons, don't I? Imagine," he said turning slightly to Nick, "I tell her she's in danger and she has to keep out of sight until I come back and what does she do? She goes to check on the barn door. It was open, you see. And she had to close it."

"You're mean," she slapped him over his arm and took her hand away.

"Mean? I am mean, did you hear her?" he asked Nick.

"I think there's much more than that here," Nick intervened in the discussion. "Adam wouldn't have been so angry if it had been a mere barn door open," he told Diane.

Diane blushed violently and Adam's lips twitched with mirth.

"Of course, there's more. She was clubbed over the head, tied up and locked in the barn. They set the barn on fire afterward and if I hadn't come when I came she'd have been barbecue," Adam remarked insensitively. "You can see the results on her face. Her hair was singed as well..."

"You're a pig, you know that," Diane cried out and tears appeared in her eyes.

She rushed past them to the kitchen and discreetly wiped her eyes. Adam took note of her gesture and sighed.

"Women are so difficult, Nick," he observed.

"Especially when you care about them," Nick replied quietly.

"What the heck do you mean?" Adam asked quarrelsome.

"Come on, bro, it's obvious. You're crazy about her and she's crazy about you. Yet, both of you go out of your way to hurt each other and keep one another to an arm's length," Nick replied and his voice sounded tired.

"I think you're too tired to think straight," Adam said. "Let me show you to your bedroom and then you can come to the kitchen, have a bite and turn in."

Adam started ahead of Nick and shook his head.

'Oh man, Nick's got barmy. Listen to him! I'm crazy about that contrary woman. And she's crazy about me.'

Suddenly, Adam stopped and tilted his head. *'Now, that's interesting. So many possibilities.'*

He shook his head to clear it and turned to Nick.

"Did you have a fine trip?"

Nick burst into laughter, and laughed heartily. He bent and pressed a hand to his midriff.

'Adam was always a wacky one,' he thought.

***

Nick had already gone to sleep. Adam had taken a shower first in the bathroom he was going to share with Nick, and now lay on the sofa, on his back, his head on his crossed hands. His legs hung over the end of the sofa. It wasn't very comfortable but he had slept in worse conditions in the past and didn't care.

Diane appeared in the doorway. The moon lit her slender figure.

"Are you all right there?" she asked him quietly.

He shrugged but then realized she couldn't see him as well as he saw her and answered, "I suppose."

She shuffled her feet. Uncertainty marred her features and Adam smiled.

Suddenly, he blurted out, "Nick says you like me. Do you?"

She froze and a blush crept all over her face and touched the tips of her ears.

"I... I... don't... know," she stammered and his grin widened.

"I see," he replied. "He said I like you too," he observed and she blinked.

After a few seconds a silence, she asked in a small voice, "Do you?"

He stared at her for a few moments and then shrugged, "I suppose."

Diane hugged herself and lowered her head. He couldn't see her face and didn't like it.

"Do you want to sleep with me?" Adam asked and her head came up with a jolt.

"What? I don't... I don't just sleep around," she managed to say.

"I didn't ask for you to sleep around. I was talking about sleeping. I know you're not like that," he chided her.

"Just sleeping?" she asked for confirmation.

Adam rolled his eyes and said, "Yes."

Diane took her time to think about it. Adam waited patiently but after a couple of minutes, he lost his patience and said in a hard voice, "Forget it."

"No," she replied. "I was just thinking we'd be more comfortable in my bedroom upstairs. You don't fit on this sofa by yourself. With me there..."

Adam stood up in a fluid move. He picked up his gun and phone off the coffee table and closed the distance between them.

"Lead the way," he said and laced his fingers through hers.

CHAPTER 13

Nick and Adam took turns to check around the ranch the entire morning. One of them always remained with Diane, although she had promised Adam not to go out if they weren't there. Adam didn't say whether he believed her or not but he didn't leave her by herself in the house either.

Nick knew where Adam had spent the night. He'd heard the two of them going upstairs the night before, and he had seen Adam coming out of Diane's room in the morning.

However, he didn't ask any personal questions. He was a very private person and he respected other people's privacy, as well.

The three of them shared a hearty lunch around one o'clock. Adam insisted on grilling some steaks and Diane gave in.

She prepared some salad, which Adam ate while grumbling. Nick enjoyed it and praised Diane for her cooking talents until Adam rolled his eyes and said, "Drop it, Nick. That's enough."

The men regaled Diane with stories from their past. Of course, they didn't go into any gory details and talked only about the funny moments they had shared together.

Diane knew they edited the stories to match with what they thought of her. She didn't mind. She actually preferred not to know the particulars.

While they were eating, Ryan sent a message to let them know they would arrive that afternoon. Adam read it and grinned.

"What's so funny?" Nick wanted to know.

"I was sure Kate wouldn't stay at home. Ryan's putty in her hands."

"Don't be so sure," Nick shook his head. "When it comes to her safety, he's anything but putty," Nick replied. "I'm sure you remember what happened before their wedding," he reminded Adam of the adventure they shared together.

"What happened?" Diane asked, her curiosity pricked.

Adam grimaced. Diane assumed he didn't want to tell her that specific story and wondered why.

Nick smiled when he noticed Adam's scowl. He leaned forward, took another slice of bread and broke it in two.

Then, he said, "I'll tell you what happened."

"Come on, man," Adam protested, but Nick waved his hand to shut him up.

"This smart guy here was lured into a trap," Nick started, pointing to Adam. "He accepted a mission on the side after we all had decided to get out of the business," Nick said with reproach, staring at Adam, who shrugged. "When we got to him, he'd already been in hiding for a while. The thing is, those guys were waiting for us. They wanted to take all of us out in an ambush. Adam got shot," Nick continued under Diane's widened eyes. "Three times, if I remember correctly," he said turning to Adam for confirmation.

"Does it matter?" Adam growled.

"Was it bad?" Diane asked in a small voice.

When Nick confirmed with a nod, she felt a twinge of pain in her heart. Unconsciously, she stroked Adam's arm.

'Maybe it's not so bad if Nick tells her the story. Oh, Gad, can I be more pathetic?' Adam mused. A moment later, he shook his head with derision and that move drew Diane's inquiring eyes. He shrugged as if it hadn't been important.

"What happened afterward?" Diane turned her attention back to Nick.

Yet, her fingers didn't stop from stroking Adam's arm. He didn't feel the need to point that out to her and decided to enjoy her ministrations.

"We had to keep a very low profile for a few weeks... Make that a few months... Adam was badly hurt and for a while there, it was touch and go. We didn't know if he'd live," Nick remembered with a scowl on his face.

Diane's fingers shook on Adam's skin and he covered them with his. He squeezed her fingers in comfort, and then pulled her hand to him. After a light kiss on her knuckles, he drew her small hand between his two big palms.

Nick pretended not to see anything and went on with his story.

"Ryan looked on Internet and connected with Kate. We needed money since we couldn't use our cards and-"

Diane jumped off her chair and interrupted him, "You mean Ryan wanted Kate to get her money?"

Her eyes widened because of the unpleasant surprise.

"It wasn't like that, for God's sake," Adam interjected and pulled her down in her chair. "Ryan had already decided to find a woman on the Internet for a relationship. And we didn't ask for her money and then ran away. We intended to give her the money back, Diane. We're not like that," he protested, a frown etched on his face. He thundered her with his eyes, finding her reaction unpleasant.

"Kate reacted exactly like you, Diane," Nick intervened with a shake of his head. "Still, she came through. She brought the money to Ryan and that actually saved all of us. They both got smitten like crazy in a matter of hours," he smiled warmly.

"Yep," Adam said. "We weren't even on the plane and he'd already asked her to marry him," he shook his head as if he couldn't understand Ryan's behavior.

Nick nudged him with his fist.

"Come on, bro, it was Ryan's best decision. They have a good marriage, I'd say, even if it's been just a little over a year."

"Yeah, it was," Adam smiled. "They're never bored and they clicked like firecrackers," he laughed.

"I wonder how they could get here so fast," Diane mused. "I thought Ryan said they were living in Montreal."

"Yeah, they live in Montreal. That's where Kate's shop is and Ryan opened a business in that area," Adam said.

"It was a smart move," Nick intervened. "He didn't have anything steady somewhere else but Kate already had her business there."

"I didn't say otherwise," Adam remarked, lifting a brow.

"Didn't say you did," Nick replied mildly. "But, yes, Diane has a point. How come they can be here so soon?"

"He said details would follow," Adam shrugged. "How could I know?"

"So, what's the plan for the afternoon?" Diane inquired to put a stop to their bickering.

"A routine check of the perimeter every two hours, I suppose," Nick ventured to say.

Adam nodded. "Exactly. I'll take the first one in about an hour and you'll take the next, all right?"

Nick agreed and they finished their lunch in silence. Reality always found a way to intrude.

The men helped Diane to clean the table and offered to do the dishes, which she accepted wholeheartedly. She felt a twinge of guilt knowing that they had their work anyway, but her guilt was short lived. It didn't last for more than a second. She wasn't very fond of doing the dishes.

She left them by the sink, Adam with his hands in the suds, and headed to the hallway.

"Hey, where are you going?" he turned and asked her.

Diane turned and stared pointedly at the water and foam dripping on the floor. Adam didn't care. A frown between his brows, he stared her down.

"Oh, for Christ's sake, I'm not leaving the house," she threw her hands in the air, frustrated with his mistrust. "I might sit on the veranda for a short-"

"Why?"

"To draw, smart guy," she replied. "I have an exposition coming up, soon enough, and I haven't done much."

"Ah, all right. Be there where I can reach you quickly," he ordered and returned to the dishes.

He could hear the wheels in her head turning and felt the heat of her frustration. A grin plopped on his lips, he continued to do the dishes meticulously.

Diane stomped out of the kitchen and Nick shook his head.

"You like to needle her, Adam."

"So what?" he shrugged.

"You might lose her if you keep it up like that," Nick replied wisely.

Adam turned to him slowly. His eyes revealed his astonishment.

"What the heck are you talking about?"

"Come on, mate, it's me, Nick. You don't have to play possum with me. It's

157

crystal clear the two of you have the hots for one another."

"So what?" Adam asked defensively. "It'll pass, you'll see," he affirmed with nonchalance.

"You try so hard not to care, it's laughable," Nick shook his head.

"Drop it, bro," Adam growled.

"If you say so," Nick replied and started drying the plates.

CHAPTER 14

At around four in the afternoon, Kate and Ryan drove into the ranch yard. Ryan drove slowly, following Adam's directions. The booby traps were still in place and he'd have preferred to get to the house in one piece.

Ryan didn't even turn off the engine that Kate got off the car and slammed the door behind her. She stomped to the stairs where Diane, Adam and Nick were waiting. Adam's eyebrows rose and Nick scowled.

Ryan followed her in long strides and caught up with her before she reached the stairs. He attempted to grab her arm, but she pulled away irately.

"Troubles in paradise?" Adam mused and Ryan sneered at him.

Nick elbowed Adam to keep his mouth shut. Adam had a talent to enrage Ryan, especially when it came to Kate.

"She lied to me," Ryan accused pointing to Kate, and his mouth tightened in a hard line.

She whirled around to him and pushed her sunglasses up so he couldn't miss the contempt in her eyes.

"I didn't lie to you, Ryan. I just didn't tell you before we left home. There's a difference," Kate replied.

"That's lying, Kate. Check the dictionary," he retorted.

"Do you have a dictionary?" Kate turned peevishly to Diane. "I want to prove this baboon that I'm right."

For a second, Diane looked like a deer caught in the headlights of a car tumbling down the freeway at full speed. She glanced at Adam and then at Nick, but they didn't help with any kind of suggestion. They just grinned.

Then, she turned back to Kate and said hesitantly, "I think there's one in the office," she pointed inside of the house. "If you want, we can check now," she proposed, unsure of what she should do.

Adam grinned. Diane's confusion showed on her face and amused him.

'She's so damn sweet,' he thought, and, for a moment, he forgot about his own hesitations. He gathered her on his side, an arm around her waist.

Diane turned her wide eyes to him and bit her lower lip. She'd thought he liked her somehow, but he was always careful to keep his distance. Last night, when he decided to sleep beside her in her bed, she thought it an aberration.

Adam squeezed her slightly. "First, I think we should find out what this discussion is about," he said and smiled at her.

"I'll tell you what's about," Ryan said heatedly. "She's pregnant," he continued in an accusatory voice, pointing his finger to Kate.

Kate just shrugged and kept a cool appearance. The others looked between

Kate and Ryan, not really understanding what was going on.

Nick recovered first and asked with a discreet cough, "And that's a problem because…"

"I thought you wanted kids," Adam jumped in. "You kept blabbering about your age and wanting kids while you could keep up with them… It was downright nauseating. So, I don't see what the problem is now."

"The problem is that she didn't tell me until we were halfway here," Ryan bellowed.

Always calm as a cucumber, Kate contradicted him, "Actually, I told you after we rented the car."

"Exactly," Ryan shouted at her.

"That's not halfway, Ryan," she explained patiently and Ryan exploded.

"Argh."

He braced his hands on his hips and turned around. He took two steps back into the yard, then came back.

"The problem is we came here to help Adam with his situation," Ryan tried to reason with her.

"So?" Kate inquired, raising her brows. "And that's a problem how?" Kate mimicked Adam's words.

"You're pregnant, woman," Ryan stated the obvious again.

"And that troubles you why?" she asked for clarifications.

"I can't have you in the middle of a situation when you're pregnant. What's so difficult to understand?" he threw his hands in the air.

"I don't see why one thing would exclude the other," she shrugged. "Anyway, we're here and we should make the best of the situation," she concluded in an icy voice.

"Yes, we're here because of you. Because you lied to me," Ryan bellowed again.

Kate just rolled her eyes and extended her hand to Diane.

"I'm Kate, by the way. The one yelling like he's lost his marbles is my *sweet* husband, Ryan. I hope we're not imposing," she inquired, shaking Diane's hand.

"No… no…" Diane stammered. "I mean I'm glad you're here. Would you like to freshen up? I could show you to your room," she offered.

"That would be fantastic. I do need some freshening up after the drive with that shouting overbearing male," she threw over her shoulder to Ryan, and practically pulled Diane into the house.

Adam grinned and Nick patted Ryan on the shoulder.

"Everything will be fine," he told him. "You'll see. We won't let anything happen to her, bro," he reassured Ryan.

Ryan nodded and hugged them both. He took a deep breath and said, "Let's talk shop."

Adam and Nick nodded and showed him the way to the kitchen. The room had become the operational center because Adam had noticed Diane had a special fondness for it.

Following Nick and Ryan into the house, Adam thought of Kate and Diane. Their physique would have confused anyone. Diane seemed to be fiery and collected at the same time, while Kate seemed very calm and warm. Yet Kate could bite someone's head off without qualms, always using that cold and controlled voice of hers.

Adam liked Kate, but he preferred Diane. She was more open. She didn't hide what she felt and she didn't step back from a hot confrontation with him. She could give as well as he could.

'Yeah, I love how she looks and I love her reactions. I love… Oh, my God,' Adam froze. He brushed his fingers through his hair and tried to come to terms with what he was about to think.

"Are you coming, mate?" Ryan inquired.

Adam didn't hear him. He was still riveted in place, contemplating his revelation.

"How the mighty fall," Nick whispered to Ryan. "I think he's just realized he's fallen hard, hook, line and sinker," he smirked. "Let's give him some privacy. We have all the time in the world later to remind him about what he said at your wedding," he laughed.

CHAPTER 15

"Mr. Monroe and his people are here, Mr. Phelps," Vera, the housekeeper, said, stopping at the threshold.

"Very well, Vera, show them in. Then, take the day off. You work hard and you deserve it," he complimented her. "I instructed Jim to drive you to Florence. You can shop and unwind for a while," he said and leaning forward, he handed her an envelope with some bills.

Vera took the envelope and the pleasure brought color in her cheeks. She murmured her thanks, hardly believing her luck.

"I don't need you until tomorrow morning around 10, so you don't have to hurry back. And Jim will keep you company," Phelps said standing up behind his desk.

He knew the middle-aged housekeeper and his driver had a thing for one another. He made his business to know everything about the people he employed. One never knew when something would come handy. Like now.

"Please, before you leave, let Duffy know that I need him and his team in here in about ten minutes."

"Yes, sir, thank you, sir," Vera replied happily, her happiness making her accent heavier.

She left in a rush, practically skipping down the hall. Phelps looked after her with condescension.

He skirted around the desk and went to pour himself a bourbon from the bar concealed behind a panel with legal books.

Phelps fancied such an oxymoron. When he was in his twenties, he kept his condoms in a box with a plump baby painted on the lid.

A knock sounded on the door. At Phelps's invitation, Monroe entered followed by his two associates, Webb and Donald.

Phelps didn't bother to glance at any of them. He sat down in an armchair next to the brown settee laid in the sitting area of his study.

He sipped his bourbon leisurely, and only when he concluded he had let them stew enough, he glanced at the three men.

They appeared uncomfortable and insecure, which Phelps had intended all along.

An ugly smile on his lips, he asked, "So, how's it going with our little business, Monroe?"

"We're still planning, sir," he said, rubbing his hands.

Phelps made him uncomfortable every time they met.

"Is that so?" Phelps asked in a hard voice. "What are you planning?"

"How to get to the woman. It's a job of finesse, sir. We need to throw the blame on that guy who lives there with her," Monroe specified.

"And how do you think you're going to do that?"

"We're still thinking of possible scenarios, sir," Monroe said and the other two nodded.

"Well, your thinking's over," Phelps replied in the same hard voice. "Three other people moved into the ranch already. Your window of opportunity's gone, Monroe," he said standing up and waving to someone behind the three. "And so are you," he said in a flat voice.

Monroe registered the threat then, but it was too late. Someone grabbed his arms from behind and coiled a rope around his wrists. He tried to fight back, but the man who was holding him was bigger and stronger.

His two companions started shouting and explaining. They ended up begging, but didn't meet with success.

Phelps signaled the men to take the three out.

"Duff," he addressed the man in charge, "I want you to dispose of them in such a way so that no one could ever trace them back to this ranch or to me."

"I've been thinking," Duff said lazily.

He scratched his head for a few seconds and chewed his tobacco. He looked everywhere but at Phelps.

"The best way is to fly them over The Rockies and set them free somewhere. I don't think anyone can trace anything on a body that crashed from 5,000 feet. Huh? What do you think?" he asked and spit on the floor.

Phelps despised Duff, but he knew he'd get the job done. He nodded his assent and his three former employees were taken out.

"I want to go over your plan about that woman tomorrow morning," he said, and Duff turned his head and acknowledged the request. "Be here at eight," Phelps ordered.

Phelps continued hearing his former employees' shouts until they had been trussed and stuffed into a trunk. He congratulated himself for having given the afternoon and evening off to the only two employees that lived on the premises.

He had expected their laments and all that begging. In a way, they made his day.

CHAPTER 16

They'd discussed the perimeter and possible ways of attack the previous evening. Adam and Nick had showed the surrounding area to Ryan.

Now, they simply patrolled the area now and then. Sometimes they made the rounds after forty-five minutes, sometimes after an hour. They didn't want to become predictable. Predictability always led to defeat.

As Kate was in the house with Diane, Adam didn't worry so much that she would take off somewhere on her own. He knew Kate wouldn't allow it and Diane didn't want to upset her.

Adam grinned. Kate knew to milk her pregnancy for all its worth. She already had Ryan eating out of her tiny palm. Nothing seemed beneath her.

When she got sick that morning, Ryan went through living hell.

As if he'd been having morning sickness, Adam thought and shook his head.

Ryan's face had been green for over half an hour.

Kate also convinced Diane not to leave her alone. She had explained that she needed constant company because she had dizzy spells and she didn't want to endanger the baby if she fell.

Adam didn't buy it. Kate must have been well enough to make Ryan take her with him. She couldn't have suddenly gotten dizzy spells.

Yet, he didn't feel like pointing that out. Kate kept Diane with her and that was what mattered to him.

Adam patrolled his side of the forest and even though he paid attention to everything, his thoughts turned to Diane all the time.

He had had a shock the day before when his feelings for Diane asserted themselves out of the blue. He had realized what Diane meant to him, and that scared the hell out of him.

Adam had never been in a relationship before. Even as a teenager, he had avoided any kind of complications and a relationship was written down as a major complication in his book.

He had dated a lot but he had never dated the same woman more than three or four times. He had also enjoyed his share of one-night stands. He always took precautions, so it didn't seem like a big deal.

His brother, James, had qualified him a cavalier man. Adam frowned remembering their last conversation. They'd shared hard words, yet, even then, Adam had known his brother was right.

James attempted to mend bridges in the letter he left for Adam with his will. He had hoped Adam would never read that letter and he would be able to tell him everything, face to face, but fate deemed it otherwise.

James had advised Adam not to be afraid of making a life for himself. He knew that their parents' skewed perception of Adam had left him in doubt of his abilities to care for someone else and assume responsibility.

Adam never liked the chores assigned to him at the ranch and did his best not to be lassoed into any kind of project his parents would plan for the farm.

He dreamed of seeing the world. He wanted a broader horizon than that small dusty ranch offered to him.

When Adam had joined the army, they had berated him. They couldn't understand why he would give up the work at the ranch. They told him he behaved like a spoiled brat who refused to grow up.

James was convinced that Adam's unwillingness to get involved with a woman, beyond sharing her bed once or twice, was a consequence of the guilt and bad-mouthing their parents had doled his way over the years.

He wrote that much in his final letter and asked Adam to understand he was his own man. He had to leave the past behind, where it belonged, and build a future for himself.

Adam hadn't thought of James's letter very often. He'd often thought of avenging him and his family but nothing else.

Diane changed all that. Her presence made him willing to believe he could have what James had urged him to build.

Adam stopped in his tracks. A slight noise from the left alerted him of an intruder. He didn't know if it was an animal or a person and decided to wait and see.

He took cover behind a wide tree trunk, his right hand on the gun in his waistband.

A whisper reached his ears, "That way, Tom."

The threat identified now, Adam crouched down, his gun in his hand, ready for attack. He didn't have to wait long. Suddenly, he found himself in a crossfire from two sides.

'*Oh, no, you don't,*' he thought. He waited for another volley of bullets to pass by him so he could accurately determine where the threat lay. Then, he started to share his bullets and had the satisfaction to hear a shout.

'*One down, two more to go,*' he thought, when another volley of bullets came his way from another angle.

It took him three tries to take out another attacker and he started enjoying himself. He had missed the adrenaline rush in his veins, such ops brought his way.

Suddenly, the forest seemed alive with shots. Adam scowled. Nick and Ryan were under fire as well.

It didn't bode well. The women were alone at the house and they were pinned down there.

Guessing their game, Adam roared with rage. He jumped up and from the cover of the tree trunk started to rain bullets in a wide circle. He took out the other gun he kept at the small of his back and fired both of them.

'*Not very smart for ammo conservation, but impossible to miss them,*' he thought.

He had plenty ammunition boxes at home, so it didn't really matter.

Adam emptied both magazines in short order and reloaded the guns. It took half of each gun to quiet the place. No one shot at him anymore.

Carefully, he advanced towards the attackers' location. He counted five bullets in the first body he encountered.

Not far away from this one he found a second man. He had been shot in the head and probably, shot a second time through his arm when he fell.

After searching the area some more, he found a third man, who was still breathing. The man tried to grab his gun and fire at Adam, but a bullet had passed through the back of his palm and he couldn't curb the hand around the gun.

"How many more?" Adam asked him in a hard voice, after he kicked the gun away.

He had grabbed the man's shirt and pulled him in a seating position. The man wheezed. Blood ran down his chin and added new splashes on his white shirt.

"How many?" Adam growled again through his teeth.

"Enough," the man said with difficulty, and then, he passed out.

Adam stood up and kicked him for good measure. He knew the man wasn't going to survive as at least one of his lungs had been perforated.

Suddenly, Adam realized the silence stretching around. No shots came from Ryan's or Nick's position. With a scowl on his face, he took out his cell phone and speed dialed Ryan.

"I'm fine," Ryan said before Adam could ask anything. "Just spoke to Nick. He's fine too."

"We have to go back to the ranch," Adam groused out. "The women are alone. I'm afraid we've fallen into a trap," Adam continued and then started cursing himself.

"I know," Ryan replied. "Calmed down. We need to keep calm now. We meet at the ranch," he said and hung off.

***

They met in the front yard of the ranch. Their faces darkened with worry when they advanced to the house. The door had been broken in and Adam's heart skipped a beat. He started running up the stairs.

Nick shook his head over his action. Adam had thrown any caution to the wind. He knew better. It could have been a trap.

Both Nick and Ryan took out their guns. Nick signaled Ryan that he should go in the back and Ryan nodded.

Nick took only a few steps when Adam's chilling roar came from inside, followed by his shout to Ryan.

"Ryan, come here, now."

Ryan's blood froze, but he forced himself to run up the stairs. His legs shook like overcooked spaghetti.

Nick forgot about caution too and followed him. Adam was alive after all, so there wasn't a trap.

They found Adam leaning over Kate in the living room. She lay on the carpet, her body coiled in a ball. She looked small, much smaller than she was.

Ryan rushed to her side and touched her face, where the blood trickled down. Anguish washed over him and his fingers shook.

Ryan felt a fist squeezing his heart. Coagulated blood had stained Kate's hair, and one of her eyes already swelled.

A second later, he noticed the blood under her nails and the shadow of a smile shook on his lips. His ferocious little kitten had taken a layer of skin off someone.

"Is she...?" Nick started to ask, but couldn't finish his question.

Ryan nodded. "Yes, she's alive. I'll still have to see the extent of her wounds, but she's breathing," he said, watching Kate's chest rise and fall rhythmically.

"That's good," Nick nodded and said with relief.

He turned around to speak to Adam, but Adam wasn't there anymore.

"Adam, where the heck did you go?" he yelled.

A door slammed upstairs and gave him the answer. Ryan and Adam looked up toward the ceiling, as if they could see through it. Another door slammed into a wall and then Adam's steps boomed down the stairs.

White-faced and disheveled, Adam appeared in the door. His eyes burnt with rage.

"They've taken her," he announced in a bleak voice.

He pushed his shaky fingers through his hair and closed his eyes. His mouth was tight and his entire body was rigid. He had failed to protect Diane and the guilt ate at his core.

Suddenly, Adam roared and hit the wall with his fist, leaving a hole behind. His knuckles bled, but he didn't notice.

"I'm going after her," he decided and with determination, he started to the door.

Nick stepped in front of him and Adam growled. "Step aside, Nick. I don't care if it's you. I'll plant my fist into your mug."

"No need for that, Adam. We will all go after Diane," he said and touched Adam's shoulder.

Adam brushed his hand off and replied, "She's my responsibility. I let her down. I have to make amends."

"How did you let her down?" Kate's weak voice came from behind him.

Adam turned to her and the light in his eyes showed that he was glad that she was conscious again.

"I'm glad you're all right, Kate," he said. "Ryan will stay with you. I have to go and get Diane."

"Where?" Ryan asked, helping Kate to sit up.

"I have my suspicions. James, my brother, told me who wanted his land. James and his family ended dead because he refused to sell. I suppose the same guy is after Diane," Adam explained.

"A Mr. Phelps?" Kate asked and all eyes turned to her with astonishment.

"How did you know?" Adam asked.

She shrugged and snuggled better in Ryan's arms. When she was comfortable enough, she continued, "They thought I was out already, so they didn't care what they said. I remained conscious enough to hear something like '*Mr. Phelps will be satisfied now. He'll get the little bitch.*' I'm sorry, Adam, that's what they said."

Adam waved her concerns away. He didn't care what those two-time pricks had said.

"What do you know about this guy?" Nick asked Adam.

"Very wealthy. Very respected and feared. I understand he has the sheriffs in about five counties in his pocket," Adam explained, rubbing his neck.

The tension had knotted his muscles and he needed to be able to move fast.

"That means very well protected," Ryan observed.

Adam just nodded and then, he shrugged.

"It doesn't matter, Ryan. I'll get to him," Adam said and turned to leave.

"Adam," Kate called him back. "I heard their thoughts. You need to be able to go in and take her. If you don't have a serious plan and die trying, she's dead as well," Kate said quietly.

Nick didn't believe Adam could get paler than he was, but he did.

"What do you mean?" he asked.

"They want to make her sign some papers. I understand they've been given a lot of leeway in that considering the methods. Their only purpose is to make her sign the ranch over to them. I read their minds. They'll kill her anyway. It doesn't matter if she signs or not," Kate explained in a sad voice.

"Okay, people, we have to think strategy here," Ryan said.

He took Kate in his arms and carried her to the sofa. He sat on the sofa and held her in his lap with care.

"Why does this man want her ranch?" he asked Adam.

"I can guess only," he replied. "James wrote that there were rumors. Phelps wanted to own this entire side of Montana. He made a lot of money being ruthless. He holds two types of hunts on his lands, and both are very expensive to attend. He's got clients who hunt exotic game and clients who hunt people."

"What are you saying?" Kate asked, her face so pale that the blood which had spotted her skin stood out.

"Real man hunt. They free one of the people they have under lock and key, usually illegal immigrants or refugees, and they hunt them with dogs and everything. Like a fox hunt if you want," Adam explained.

"Oh, my God, Ryan, you've got to do something!" Kate shouted, shocked to hear that such things were real.

"We'll do, don't worry Kate. We'll end this enterprise right now. Did they say they'd take Diane at this Phelps's house?" he asked her and smoothed her hair over the head.

"Yes, that's what they said," she nodded.

"I understand. All right," Ryan addressed Adam and Nick, "I think we'd better call Mark."

"I don't have time to wait for Mark, man," Adam replied furiously. "Diane will be dead by the time he comes."

"We won't wait for him, but we'll need him in the end, Adam. We're going to attack a very wealthy man. And we'll definitely take him down and end his illegal activities. We need back up for that, Adam," Ryan tried to reason with his friend.

"All right, then," he accepted. "But make it fast. I want to leave now," Adam replied in a steely voice. He barely held himself in check. He just wanted to go and hunt the man responsible for Diane's kidnapping.

Ryan nodded. He understood Adam's state of mind and tension. He admitted that he would have been in the same state if those goons had taken Kate.

"Adam, while I talk to Mark, will you help Kate go upstairs and clean all this blood? I'd like to see the extent of your wounds, baby," he told her and stroked her arm with tenderness.

Ryan also hoped that giving Adam something to do might forestall his impatience. He counted on Adam's protective side. Adam wasn't aware that he had one, but Ryan had seen it time and time again.

"Don't worry, Ryan, I'm fine. I just got punched in the face when I didn't sit still to tie me down. That's when I got this cut here above my eye," she said and touched the spot gingerly.

She grimaced at the touch. The spot was sore and still hurt.

"Only one guy attacked me, and believe me, he regretted it. The entire left side of his face is slashed to ribbons. You see, these nails are good for something after all," she waved her fingers before Ryan's eyes and smiled.

Ryan squeezed her fingers and kissed them. He nodded to Adam who helped Kate up and led her upstairs.

Ryan looked after them for a few seconds, and then dialed Mark's number. He explained the situation to Mark and told him what he intended to do.

CHAPTER 17

Diane was tied to a chair in the middle of one of Phelps's barns. Her upper lip had split and blood had left a trail down her chin.

She knew a bruise of a man's fist will appear on her right cheekbone later. It hurt badly, but the ache was one of many and didn't matter so much.

Phelps sprawled in a chair brought from the house. He indulged in a glass of bourbon and a satisfied smile fluttered on his lips when he looked at her.

Four other men were standing around her. They all looked at Phelps, waiting for his orders.

"So, Ms. MacLean, we finally meet. You caused me a lot of problems and I'm afraid you'll have to pay for that," he said in a hard voice.

He sipped from his glass again, thinking to let her squirm for a little while. People dreaded the unknown.

Early in his career, he had learnt not to show his cards too soon in the game and he had never strayed from that principle.

Diane just watched him and tried to steady her breathing. One of her ribs was probably cracked because it hurt every time she breathed in deeply.

"This business would have been concluded some time ago if you only had the decency to answer to my letter," Phelps observed.

Befuddled, Diane stared at him.

"Letter? What letter?"

"Don't play dumb with me, missy," his voice whipped. "You know very well I sent you a letter and offered to buy the ranch. I even offered you a reasonable price," he mentioned.

"I haven't received any letter," Diane shook her head and regretted it immediately.

She hadn't recovered completely from the blow she had received at the back of her skull the previous day. To make things worse, one of the thugs had snapped her head to the floor when they came after her. Her head hurt and every sudden move made her dizzy.

"Don't lie to me," the man bellowed and stood up in a huff.

"I'm not lying," Diane said quietly.

Phelps, already annoyed with her stubbornness, stomped toward her and slapped her face, cracking her bottom lip, as well.

Diane whimpered but then she bravely looked at him and repeated mulishly, "I'm not lying. You can hit me again if you like, but that won't change the facts."

His small eyes narrowed even more. He assessed her for a few moments, and then, he waved his hand.

"It doesn't really matter. What matters is that you sign this paper here," he showed her a piece of paper.

Her eyebrows went up interrogatively. When he didn't elaborate, she asked, "What paper's that?"

"Why, it's the paper through which you sell me the ranch and all the land," he replied, an ugly grin on his thin lips.

"I don't think so," she retorted.

"Oh, you will, don't worry. Duff, she's yours. You can stop when she signs," Phelps nodded toward Duff and left the paper on the chair.

He left the barn without looking back at her.

The fine hairs at her neck stood up. Fear trekked the length of her spine and she felt her insides shaking.

Duff cracked his knuckles and the noise attracted her eyes. The savage satisfaction in his eyes chilled her, and her eyes widened with terror.

Duff smiled at her and crossing the space between them, backhanded her and she fell backward and of course, as she was tied to the chair, she took it with her. She yelped and, for a moment, she saw red spots before her eyes.

Two of the men approached and straightened the chair. One of them pulled her hair hard and her head fell back. A groan flew off her lips, but that wasn't the end. Duff backhanded her again and she lost consciousness.

***

With the help of the night goggles, Adam had packed when he came to Montana, they assessed the number of guards around Phelps's property. Nick indicated two on the right side of the yard and Adam found four in the back.

Ryan found it interesting when he noticed two guys smoking and talking in front of a barn. The barn was lit, which was strange at that time of the night.

He elbowed Adam and showed the barn to him. Adam checked it out and nodded. He was sure Diane was kept in there.

"You take the barn, Adam," Ryan whispered. "Nick, you take care of the guards, one after another. I don't want to hear a sound until the perimeter is secured. I'll go into the house, all right?" he asked.

Adam and Nick nodded.

"You're sure Kate will be fine?" Adam asked Ryan.

He didn't want to sacrifice Kate for Diane. He knew that Diane wouldn't have ever forgiven him if he had let that happen.

"She'll be fine. She's got two guns with her and she's very well hidden," Ryan reassured him. "You know I wouldn't let anything to happen to her and she's already been hurt once today."

Adam nodded and crawled away. He would have loved to run to the barn and free Diane at once, but he knew he needed to be patient. One wrong move, and he could lose her forever.

It took him some time until he reached the side of the barn. It felt like an eternity and it strained his patience.

He advanced slowly and tried to block out the words that came from the barn and especially, Diane's cries. Every time he heard her cries, something acid burnt in his stomach. His lips were tight and his back teeth locked because of the fury which ate at him.

Adam reached the side of the building and listened carefully. Only one man paced outside the barn and the smell of smoke from a cigarette itched at his nostrils.

'There's one more inside now,' he thought.

Adam patiently waited until the man got closer. When the sound of the man's steps let him know that he was just a foot away, Adam slipped behind him.

He covered the man's mouth and nose with one hand and the back of his head with the other. The man froze, and Adam just twisted his head in a practiced move. The man's neck snapped like a twig. Adam dragged him quietly on the side of the barn and laid him there in a shadow.

'One out, God knows how many more to go,' he thought.

With silent steps, he advanced to the door. Light filtered through a crack and he looked inside.

His blood boiled instantly when his eyes fell on Diane's bloody face. A sturdy man punched her in her midriff and she whimpered again.

Adam fought hard to regain his calm. He had to take Diane out of there and he needed all his focus on that. He could take care of her afterward.

He counted four men inside. He took out his gun and installed a silencer on the muzzle. He had one shot for each and in fast succession. If he was one second too slow, Diane could end up dead.

He tightened his mouth and pulled the door open. The second the door opened and the first man turned to him, he fired. He didn't stop firing until the last one was down.

The man behind Diane tried to pull her head back and probably, snap her neck. He was Adam's second target. It was a clean shot. The bullet crossed his skull and lodged into one of the boards behind him.

When he fell, he pulled Diane down too, by her hair. Adam ignored that until he finished off the other two men, as well.

Then, he rushed to Diane, untied her and smoothed her hair away. Her teary big green eyes stared at him in wonder.

Adam cradled her in his arms and whispered, "Don't look at me like that, sweetie pie. I don't deserve it. I didn't protect you, as I should have."

Her mouth opened and for a few seconds she couldn't say anything. Then, with her last strength, she punched him in his arm and said, "Are you out of your mind? You saved my life, you lunatic. They'd have killed me if you hadn't come," she said.

He just shook his head and stood up with her in his arms.

"We'll have to get out of here first, Diane. I will check you out once we're in the clear, all right?"

She nodded and closed her eyes. A satisfied sigh flew off her lips when she nuzzled him, and his scent enveloped her.

CHAPTER 18

That night and the following morning were full of frantic activity. Ryan had restrained Phelps, who started threatening and throwing important names left and right. Ryan didn't bother to listen to him.

By the time Adam came out with Diane, Nick had already annihilated all the guards, and beside the men Adam had killed, everyone else was alive and secured to be sent to prison.

Ryan verified every prisoner, intent on finding the one who had hurt Kate. He wanted him so badly that he could taste revenge. Yet, his wish remained unfulfilled. Adam had already taken care of him.

They knew the sheriff was on Phelps's payroll, so they didn't bother to call him. They just waited for Mark's people.

They arrived just ten minutes after everything ended. Mark had sent a team from Bozeman by plane. They had landed in Missoula and driven to Phelps's property at full speed.

They were armed with search warrants, based on Kate's and Diane's accounts. Apparently, they had had their eyes on Phelps for some time but nothing had ever stuck to him and they couldn't make a move.

They checked every crack and niche in the house, and found enough evidence to burry Phelps and his associates in prison for life.

Adam, Nick and Ryan left them do their job and they drove the women to the hospital. There, they requested to have both women checked and patched out.

Kate bristled when she heard the term *patched out* in relation to her, but she relented and was satisfied to hear that her baby was still in good shape, untouched by the goon that had attacked her.

Diane hadn't been so lucky, and the doctor decided to keep her in the hospital for observation, at least for one night. She had two cracked ribs, several lacerations at the level of the face and she was bruised almost everywhere.

Adam had been terrified when he became aware of the extent of her wounds and bruises. At Diane's request, the doctor allowed him in the examination room and every time he learned about a new bruise or wound, he died a little inside.

Diane didn't want to stay there, but she accepted when Adam promised to spend the night by her side.

***

"I want to go home, Adam," Diane squeezed his hand and pleaded with her green eyes.

Adam was aware she made good use of her charms in order to bend him to her will, but he couldn't have denied her anyway.

"All right, Diane, I will talk to the doctor. If everything is fine, I'm sure he'll let you come home," he promised and kissed her forehead.

Diane's eyes flared with anger. "I'm not a child, Adam, to placate me. I'm telling you I'm fine and I want to go home. If you don't want to help, just say so and I will take care of that," she said mulishly.

"Sweetie pie, of course I want to help. And I definitely want you home," he whispered and touched her bottom lip with the tip of his finger. "But I won't do anything to jeopardize your health," he said in an implacable voice and his hard eyes held hers with determination.

"But-"

"No buts, Diane," he shushed her. "I died a thousand times knowing you were in danger. I won't go through that again," he replied stubbornly.

Diane's heart sang when she understood the meaning of his words. She only hoped he would remember them when everything had quieted down.

***

Luckily, the doctor signed her papers and she was able to check out the hospital. Adam drove her home, with a slight detour to buy some coffee and pastries for both of them. Hospital food hadn't been very appetizing and both were famished.

When he stopped the car in the yard, everybody came out to hug them and rejoice that everything had ended well.

Ryan and Nick had already disarmed Adam's booby traps because they couldn't spend all their time giving indications to the agents coming by.

"Good to have you both home," Ryan said with a smile in his voice.

He hugged Diane carefully with one arm, so he wouldn't hurt her ribs. Then he kissed the top of her head, while hugging Adam with his other arm.

"Payback is a bitch, Ryan," Adam observed. "I should do to you what you did to Nick and me when we met Kate for the first time," he joked and elbowed his friend.

Ryan laughed, but his eyes promised all sorts of punishments to Adam. He didn't like to be reminded about his jealous behavior at that time. In retrospect, he realized he had been way over the line and he felt ashamed of how he had reacted.

They went inside and gathered around the kitchen table. Kate and Nick brought mugs with hot coffee at the table while Ryan brought Adam up to speed.

The agents had already found one camp with locked people and one with exotic animals. Phelps wouldn't ever see the light of day out of a prison cell.

Ryan doubted he would see it inside a cell for long either. Apparently, many important people were involved in Phelps's scheme. Some of them would certainly try to get rid of the most important witness against them, so Phelps's days were counted.

Phelps had liked to show his power and muscles when he dealt from a strong position. Now, that he was under arrest without the possibility for bail, he sang like a canary. He didn't like the idea of going down by himself but seemed determined to bring down with him as many people as possible.

After discussing the case, they began talking about mundane things. The men shared funny memories to entertain the ladies and mocked one another. Diane and Kate enjoyed their antics and the strong bond between them.

"I'm thinking of going back home," Nick said. "I don't really like having other people taking care of my horses," he confessed.

"Stay at least until tomorrow," Diane begged him. "We'll have a nice barbecue, exactly the way Adam likes it," she winked at him, although it wasn't easy. Her right eye had swelled badly and the left one was just a little better.

"She's right," Adam agreed. "I'm sure you'll survive if you stay one more day."

Nick pondered their invitation but in the end, he accepted, although his heart cringed at the thought that someone else looked after his horses.

"What are you going to do now, Adam?" Kate asked.

He shrugged.

"I'm not very sure. I was thinking of teaching some survival courses. I understand they work fine."

"Not a bad idea," Ryan said, thumping him over the shoulder. "You're good at survival, so I can see you being a success."

"That's what I thought," Adam nodded. "And I was also thinking of marrying Diane," he blurted out and everyone was rendered speechless.

Diane's eyes widened and shone with unshed tears. She stared at him, unable to utter one word.

Kate punched him in the arm, "You scamp, is that how you ask a woman to marry you? You're one brick short of a full load, Adam," she shook her head with reproach. "I'd club him over the head if I were you," she told Diane.

Adam frowned for a few seconds, not understanding what came over her. He didn't find anything amiss in what he had said. Then, the truth dawned over him.

'Oh, right," Adam said and slapped his forehead. "Women want romance. Do you want romance, Diane?" he asked her, an eyebrow hitched up on his forehead.

Diane didn't answer. Poleaxed, she just kept looking at him.

Ryan put his head in his hands and Nick shook his head. Adam looked from one to the other and another truth dawned on him.

"I blew it, didn't I?" he asked Diane. "Sweetie pie, I don't have any experience with this romance stuff. Never been romantic before. If I go and buy you some flowers and a box of chocolates and come back and kneel before you, will you say yes?"

Wide-eyed, Diane still stared at him and said nothing.

"Oh, for God's sake, give a guy a break. I love you, isn't it enough?" he shouted and threw his hands in the air.

Kate and the guys burst into laughter.

"You're pathetic, man," Ryan said, shaking his head. "Not even I could have made more of a mess of a marriage proposal than you."

Adam didn't pay any attention to any of them. He kept looking at Diane.

She finally nodded and said, "Yes, Adam, it's enough. I don't need the flowers and chocolates."

That's what he expected to hear.

"Hurrah!" he shouted and jumping off the chair, he pulled Diane up into his arms and started spinning her around.

Despite her aching ribs, she burst into laughter. Her happiness filled the room and fed the others' joy.

EPILOGUE

Diane and Adam married on Christmas Day. Diane had always dreamed to have a white wedding: white dress, white flowers, snow on the road and on the roof.

Kate and Ryan came for the wedding from Montreal even though Ryan grumbled about Kate's exhaustion. Luckily for him, Kate had already stopped paying attention to his excessive care because of her pregnancy.

Nick asked someone to take care of his horses and came together with Mark, their former boss.

When the bride walked along the aisle, holding Nick's arm, Adam's eyes shone with tears and the sight made everyone smile. They remembered well what he had declared at Ryan's wedding and couldn't stop making fun of him whenever they had a chance.

The bride wore a simple coronet of weaved white flowers and her dress had turned her into a princess. She sauntered toward Adam with elegant and graceful steps.

'*My princess,*' Adam thought, when he took her hand in his and kissed her palm.

After they said the '*I dos*', he impatiently waited until the pastor declared them husband and wife. Then, he kissed her hard, leaving her breathless.

After his lips left hers, he stared into her eyes and whispered '*Hurrah!*' Her eyes danced with joy and satisfaction.

When he lifted her in his arms and strode out of the church to the car with huge strides, her laughter joined the others'.

The snow had covered the road and the smell of pines filled the air. Adam kissed her hard again, opened the car door and sat her inside.

Without a single look at their guests, he drove her away, up the road to their ranch, under the stunned eyes of the people who came out of the church.

They knew a wedding feast was waiting for them at the ranch, but they had believed that the bride and the groom would wait for them.

Laughing, Ryan slapped Nick on the back and said with enthusiasm, "Your turn now, mate."

Nick shook his head and shuddered with apprehension. *'Not in this lifetime if I can help it'*.

Author's Bio

Rowena Dawn writes romance, reads thrillers and watches comedies. She likes walking through the woods but insanely loves the sea.

She has a love - hate relationship with her writing and drives her dog crazy whenever she doesn't stop writing to take him out.

This series *Perfect Halves* will have four books and all of them will be about love, adventure and conspiracies. You have met all male characters in the first novel, **Double-Edged** and this second novel, **Eyes in the Dark.**

Look for Book Three in Rowena Dawn's *"Perfect Halves"* series: **PULLED IN.** Coming soon!

Also by Rowena Dawn:

Double-Edged – Book One in The Perfect Halves Series – eBook, paperback (soon audio book)

Leap of Faith – eBook, paperback (soon audio book)

Becka's Awakening (Book One in The Winstons Series) – eBook, paperback and audio book

Mr. (Almost) Right eBook, paperback and audio book

Thank you for taking the time to read *EYES IN THE DARK*, the second book in the series **The Perfect Halves**.

If you enjoyed it, please consider telling your friends or posting a short review.

Word of mouth is an author's best friend and much appreciated. Thank you,

Rowena Dawn